Spotted Pony Casino Mysteries

Poker Face
House Edge

D1553934

House Edge

Spotted Pony Casino Mystery
Book 2

Paty Jager
Windtree Press

HOUSE EDGE

Contact Information: info@windtreepress.com

Windtree Press
Hillsboro, Oregon
http://windtreepress.com

Cover Art by Covers by Karen

PUBLISHING HISTORY
Published in the United States of America
ISBN 978-1-957638-01-0

About this series

This series is set in and around a fictional casino on The Confederated Tribes of the Umatilla Reservation in NE Oregon. The reservation is real. I have researched, and while I've made up people and where they live, I will try to stay true to the life people live on the reservation.

The casino is modeled a little bit after the real Wildhorse Casino at the reservation. But I changed some things around. The operations of the casino in my series are all my own common sense, not a complete knowledge of how any casino is run.

A Special Thank you to:

Lieutenant Dan Conner of the Oregon State Police and Umatilla Tribal Police Chief Tim Addleman for answering my questions.

Chapter One

"How could you do this to my family. My People?"

Dela Alvaro, head of security for the Spotted Pony Casino, moved closer to the gaming tables. Surveillance had reported there was a couple at the blackjack table arguing more than they were playing. That usually meant they were trying to draw attention away from someone else stealing.

"It's not a done deal," the well-dressed man in his thirties, said. He had a clean-shaven face and a loosened necktie. He looked familiar, but she couldn't place where she'd seen him.

"You are like a brother to them. How could you?" The woman's heart-shaped face had deep lines of frustration embedded in her forehead.

A crowd had started to gather. There was nothing the locals liked better than to watch a soap opera being played out by non-rez casino goers.

"Stacy, I want a good future for us." The man grabbed the woman's wrist. His fingers slid off as she jerked her arm away.

"There is no future if you go through with what your company wants over what the People need." She spun on her heels and ran for the elevator, shouting at someone in the conveyance to hold the door.

The man who had argued with the woman scanned the area and strode toward the elevator.

Dela spoke into the mic clipped to her shirt. "Anyone know that couple?"

"He's part of the summit going on this week," a voice through her earbuds said.

She walked over to the entrance of the event center and picked up a flyer from the table stationed by the poster for the SAVE OUR FISH event. The photo on the front of the flyer matched the man. Kevin Silva, executive VP of environment, fish and wildlife, with the Hells Canyon Power Company in Idaho. The summit was about breaching four dams in Idaho to help the dwindling salmon, steelhead, and lamprey populations.

Dela had read about this situation in the local and tribal newspapers. The fish that would be aided by taking out the dams had been food staples for the Indigenous People of the Pacific Northwest for generations. Fish and Wildlife agencies had tried everything, including building state-of-the-art fish hatcheries to keep the fish population up, but even that wasn't working. They were down to drastic measures that many people didn't like.

Pulling out her cell phone, Dela dialed Shona White, the events coordinator for the casino.

"Hello?" Shona answered.

"Shona, it's Dela. Can you tell me if Kevin Silva checked into the hotel with anyone?"

"Yes. His wife, Stacy. We had a brief conversation. She is Nez Perce and Coeur d'Alene."

"Did they seem to be getting along when you met them?" Dela wondered at the falling out they had tonight at the gaming tables. Did the husband gamble too much?

"Oh, they were loving and seemed to be making the most of this trip."

"Thank you."

Dela put her phone away and returned to her nightly duties. It appeared something had happened to change the tone of the couple's trip.

As head of security for the Spotted Pony Casino, Dela didn't have to be at the casino on busy nights. She could have kept the same daytime schedule as her predecessor, but she felt she was needed more during the busy hours than when the casino floor was slow.

It was eleven p.m. and other than the argument at the blackjack table, this Wednesday night had been uneventful. Going home sounded like a good option. Mugshot would be happy to see her so early and it would give her a chance to check out the work Travis and his crew did today on her house.

She never worked the same hours. It kept everyone, especially her security staff, on their toes. As long as she was on a salary, she made her own schedule and worked as many hours as she wanted.

Dela entered the security office and opened the cabinet by her desk. She pulled out her purse.

"You going home?" Marie asked.

Dela faced the security officer standing at the entrance where employees, off-site technicians, and deliveries came through at the back of the building. "Yes. It's quiet and Kenny is here. I have a dog waiting for me at home."

She walked over, tapped her security card on the keypad, and the door opened.

"Enjoy what's left of your night," Marie said, as Dela exited.

"I will." Thoughts of a cold beer, putting her stub up, and petting Mugshot made her smile.

On the three-mile drive to her "new to her" home, she envisioned what she would find. She'd been looking for a place to rent when she and FBI Agent Quinn Pierce drove to Tutuilla Flats to question a murder suspect a few months earlier. She'd spotted a rundown house for sale and knew it was the perfect place for her and Mugshot. She'd just acquired the pony-sized, three-legged dog and needed a place for him to hang out while she was at work.

The one and a half acres were more than she needed, but it kept her neighbors at a distance. There was no need for someone to call the police if she yelled out in frustration over her missing lower right leg.

Pulling up to the house, the outdoor light came on. Travis had insisted she needed motion detector lights so all those late nights she came home from the casino, the lights would come on for her to get from the car to the house.

Mugshot's happy bark greeted her as she walked up to the front door and let herself in. She dropped her purse on the only chair in the living room and walked straight over to the French doors Travis had installed in place of the large paned sliding door in the dining room area.

She unlocked and opened the door.

Mugshot shoved his head, the size of a basketball, against her and waited for her to scratch his ears and tell him he was a good boy. Then he stepped into the house and made his way to the large dog bed next to the chair.

Her mother had been afraid the dog would knock her over, and the two amputees would be hurt. But Mugshot seemed to understand that she couldn't hold him up if he fell and while he liked to be scratched and hugged now and then, he made certain to stay out of her way.

"I'm going to get changed and grab something to drink, then I'll be right there." She went into the bedroom, undressed, took off her prosthesis, and put on her pajamas. Then she used her crutches to return to the kitchen, get a beer and a box of crackers, and settle in the chair. Placing her refreshments on the side table, she picked up the TV controls and turned on a murder mystery show. She ate her snack while petting Mugshot and watching the mind-numbing television.

♠ ♣ ♥ ♦

The ring of her phone and Mugshot nudging her arm woke Dela. She patted the dog's head as she reached for the phone.

"Dela," she answered and glanced at the clock. The red numbers revealed 10:00. The sun reflected through the shade she kept drawn in this room.

"It's Bruce. Housekeeping has reported a dead person in room ten-twenty."

She sat up and scrubbed a hand over her face.

"Who is it?"
"The occupant. Kevin Silva."

Chapter Two

Dela arrived at room 1020 as Tribal Police Detective Jones stepped out into the hallway. She loathed the Caucasian man because of his disregard for Indigenous culture and the way he treated everyone around him. She'd heard rumors he was retiring. It wouldn't be soon enough for her.

"I wondered when you'd show up," he said.

"Got here as quick as I could after receiving the call." She wasn't about to tell him that on the way in, she'd talked to Bruce and had been filled in on how Rae, in housekeeping, found the body and that they couldn't find the wife anywhere on the premises.

"There was no need for you to hurry down. We have this under control."

A tribal officer leaned out of the room and studied her. "Dela, good to see you made it. You might want to take a look around."

She did a double-take, then smiled. Heath Seaver, a

person she hadn't seen since high school. Grandfather Thunder had said his nephew was moving back to the reservation.

She smiled at Detective Dick, as she called him, and followed her former classmate into the room. Dela waved a hand up and down in front of him. "I didn't even know you were a policeman, and here you are dressed in a tribal uniform."

Heath grinned and she couldn't stop smiling back at him. They had dated their junior year. He'd been the closest thing to a confidante she'd had back then. She'd had girls who were friends and were still friends to this day, but she hadn't told any of them how she yearned to know more about her father. Heath had understood. He also grew up not knowing his father. His mother refused to talk about the man.

"Not just a tribal policeman, I'm also a certified MDI." He pulled latex gloves on and handed her a pair.

"You are a Medicolegal Death Investigator? I knew they had hired someone who had that capability." She pulled the gloves on.

"I've already called the Pendleton Office." He motioned toward the body still sitting in a chair.

By the Pendleton Office, he meant the FBI. It wouldn't be long and she'd be facing FBI Special Agent Quinn Pierce. She still owed the man a visit to her new home. She'd offered him an open invitation, but every time he'd called, she came up with an excuse to keep him away. Dela knew it was cowardice, but she was afraid if she let him in, she'd like it too much and she wasn't ready to tell this particular man all of her secrets.

"Dela?" Heath stood in front of her, waving his

hand back and forth before her face.

"Sorry. My mind wandered."

Heath studied her for a few seconds and handed her the little booties everyone else in the room had on.

She slipped the paper covers over her shoes and moved farther into the room.

Heath motioned toward the victim. "I understand he and his wife had a fight down in the casino last night?"

"Yes." She focused on the body. "The conversation didn't make any sense." She stood as close as she could without possibly stepping on evidence. The man's face was puffy as well as his neck down to where there was an electrical cord dangling from the indention in his neck. The man had been handsome in life. In death, he was hard to look at. "Strangulation?"

"Yeah. With the cord from that lamp." He nodded toward the table. The cord was still attached to the lamp.

"Premeditated or spur of the moment?" she asked.

"I'd say spur of the moment, but we won't know until you figure it out."

She shot a glance at the tall, Indigenous man, smiling down at her. His smile was infectious, but she didn't understand his comment. "I'm not the police."

"But you seem to get wrapped up in anything that happens at the casino. Grandfather Thunder told me all about the missing women, the human traffickers, and the body shoved in the laundry chute. He said you solved all of them."

"With help." Quinn's deep voice pulled her gaze from Heath's handsome face to the special agent's.

"That's true. Special Agent Pierce was kind

enough to drive me around so I could gather the evidence." Dela walked over to the closet to see if the wife had taken her clothing with her when she'd left. As she studied the contents, she kept one eye on the two men, now sizing each other up.

"Special Agent Quinn Pierce," the FBI agent said, holding his hand out to Heath.

"Heath Seaver, MDI with the Tribal Police."

They shook and Quinn walked over to stand beside Dela who'd ducked into the bathroom. "What do you know about the victim?"

She glanced at the sink, countertop, and shower before stepping out of the room. Watching Heath do his job, she relayed why the victim was at the casino, what she'd witnessed the night before, and the fact there were still women's clothing in the closet but no toiletries in the bathroom.

"Do you think the wife did this and ran?" Quinn asked.

Dela shook her head slowly. "I didn't get the vibe she was that angry. She was more disappointed. Like he'd let her down."

"I had my guys look up info on the couple when I received the call. Mrs. Silva has family on the reservation. Let's go see if that's where she ran off to." Quinn motioned for her to leave the room as another tribal police officer joined the group in the room collecting evidence.

They were halfway to the elevator when Heath caught up to them. "I'll let you know what else the medical examiner finds when she signs off on the body. I'll transport the body to Clackamas and stay for the autopsy there."

Quinn stopped. "What authority do you have to go with the body?"

Heath grinned. "Detective Jones told me to discover all I could about the body. You can join me if you want."

Quinn glared at Heath. "I don't have time to run across the state to watch the autopsy. Just see the body is brought back and I get a copy of the report."

Heath saluted Quinn, winked at Dela, and ducked back into the room. Dela suppressed a snicker. That was the Heath she remembered in school. Always thumbing his nose at authority. Which brought her to, how had he ended up in law enforcement?

"You could give me the information on Mrs. Silva's family, then you could go with Heath to the Oregon State Medical Examiner's Office." Dela held her phone in her hands ready to type in the address or name of the family.

Quinn studied her. "You find this amusing that someone is undermining me, don't you?"

"A little. How's it feel to be treated as if your work doesn't matter?" She knew it was petty to bring up the event in Iraq that had her hating Quinn for a long time.

"Are you ever going to see I did what I did because it was my duty?" Quinn asked, grasping her arm.

They'd talked this to death and it still irked her. Dela shook out of his hold and changed the subject. "I'm sure if Heath has been trained as one of the tribal MDI, he is capable of escorting the body and standing in on the autopsy." She glanced back at the room where the man had disappeared. When Grandfather Thunder had told her his nephew was coming to work at the reservation, she'd been pleased to know she would have another friend in the area. Now she wished Quinn was going with the body so she and Heath could catch up.

"Do you know him?" Quinn asked as they stopped at the elevator.

"We went to school together. He is a nephew of Grandfather Thunder. I knew he was coming to work at the reservation. I just didn't know he was in law enforcement."

That seemed to appease Quinn. He punched the button for down, and they waited. "How come you always blow me off when I have time to come see your new place?" He continued to stare at the elevator door.

Her gut tumbled. "Because I'm busy. It's still not ready for guests." And she didn't want him to see the shiny new handicapped bars in the bathroom.

"I know you are remodeling. You saw my house in its worst state. I'm not expecting it to be perfect."

The door opened and they stepped in.

She sighed. "I'm not ready for anyone to see how I live."

His eyebrow went up. "See how you live? Do you live some kind of kinky life I don't know about?"

She glared at him. "In your dreams. I'm just not ready to share all of my life with anyone yet."

"I'm not asking you to marry me. Just let me see what you've done to the house." He stared at her.

"My life is complicated and so is how I live." The elevator settled on the ground floor and she stepped out. "Where are we going?"

"The Rose family out near Wildhorse Mountain," Quinn said, as they strode across the casino floor. He kept his stride restrained to not overtake her.

"That would be Melba and Butch. How are they

related to Mrs. Silva?" Dela nodded to the daytime valet. If Alfred, the nighttime valet, were still on duty, they'd know more about the couple. He had a keen sense of people and watched everything.

Quinn walked to his SUV. "Mrs. Silva is their niece by marriage or something like that."

They climbed in and he drove off, headed north to Highway 11. About thirteen miles on Highway11 they made a right onto Wildhorse Road.

"Did you happen to find anyone who could tell you this is where she went?" Dela wondered if the woman had been so upset with her husband she'd left before he was killed. But she could have also killed her husband and left as well. Wildhorse Mountain was a good forty-five minutes from the casino.

Quinn's phone rang. He answered it through the vehicle. "Special Agent Quinn. You're on speaker. I have Dela Alvaro, head of security at the casino, with me."

"You asked for information on the Silvas." The agent went on to say who the man worked for and how much the company would lose if the dams were breached and how the company had been trying to get a better name for itself.

"What about the wife?" Dela asked when the agent had stopped reading the report.

"She has her own business. The couple met ten years ago and have been married for seven years. No children. Her family is for the breaching and some have picketed the power company with signs stating the need to bring back the First People's food sources."

"Any priors for either of them?" Quinn asked.

"Nothing that we could find. They are both

upstanding citizens."

"Thanks." Quinn ended the call. "What makes two 'upstanding citizens' snap and one kill the other?"

Dela stared at him. "Don't be so quick to condemn the wife. If they haven't had any trouble up till now, why would she snap over one little disagreement?"

"Why does any woman go psycho?" He glanced at her.

"Are you calling me psycho?" She pointed to the road they needed. "Turn left there."

"You invited me to come by your place and then when I try, you refuse. That's just a bit psycho to me." Quinn glanced at her.

"Can we just work on this murder? I don't have the time or energy to verbally battle with you." She stared forward. She didn't want him badgering her the whole time they worked to solve Mr. Silva's murder.

"I know when to back off." He parked in front of an older house with peeling paint and moss growing on the shingles.

Dela glanced at him before sliding out of the vehicle. She'd upset him. Sheesh. He really needed to lose the ego. She walked up to the door and knocked.

A chorus of barking could be heard inside the house.

The door opened. An older Umatilla woman with silver in her braided hair peered out at them through film-covered eyes. "Hello?"

"Mrs. Rose?" Dela asked.

"Yes, I'm Melba Rose. Who are you?"

"I'm Dela Alvaro and this is Special Agent Pierce. We'd like to speak to Mrs. Silva."

"Stacy? Why would you need to speak to her?"

The woman didn't open the door any further.

"Please, it's important. It's about her husband," Dela said, surprised Quinn hadn't butted in.

"Kevin? What has he been saying about our Stacy?" The woman became offensive.

"Nothing. Please may we speak to Stacy?" Dela glanced over the woman's shoulder and spotted an older gentleman holding three old dogs that appeared to be part chihuahua in his arms.

"Melba, let them in," the man said.

The woman reluctantly opened the door wider.

Dela and Quinn stepped inside the living room as a man, in his thirties, dressed in a flannel shirt and jeans walked in from what appeared to be the kitchen.

"Who are you?" he asked, visibly bristling as he glared at them.

This time Quinn made the introductions.

The man glared at Quinn. "Fed? Why are you looking for Stacy?"

"Could you please have Mrs. Silva come into the living room?" Dela asked the old woman.

Mrs. Rose shuffled down the hall.

Dela rested her weight on her left leg, giving her stub a rest, and waited.

The old woman returned. "She'll be out. She's getting dressed."

It was close to 1 pm. Why hadn't the woman felt like dressing? Was she emotionally overwrought from, oh say, killing her husband?

"What time did Mrs. Silva arrive here last night?" Quinn asked as if he'd had the same thought.

"I picked her up when she called," the younger man said.

"And you are?" Quinn pulled out a notepad.

"Ben Gibbons." The man leaned against the doorway into the kitchen.

"Why would Mrs. Silva call you?" Dela asked.

"She didn't. She called grandma, and she asked me to pick Stacy up."

The old woman smiled at the younger man. "He's a good grandson. He helps us out."

"How are you related to Mrs. Silva?" Quinn asked.

"We're distant cousins." Ben crossed his arms.

"It had been years since I'd seen Ben, but the minute I laid eyes on him, I knew he was Melba's grandson." Mrs. Silva walked into the living room dressed in a tunic top and pants that weren't quite bellbottoms but had some flare at the bottom of the legs.

She held out her hand. "I'm Stacy Silva. Why are you looking for me? I'm sure Kevin figured out this is where I went when I said I needed some space to think."

Dela exchanged glances with Quinn. When he started to open his mouth, Dela held up a hand. "Mrs. Silva, I'm sorry to inform you that your husband is dead."

The woman's eyes widened. She sucked in a breath before collapsing on the couch. "No! We have plans. He can't…" She hugged her arms around herself as Ben sat down beside her, putting an arm around her shoulders.

The woman stared at the wall across from her. "We argued last night. I overheard someone thank him for his support for not breaching the dams." She slid her gaze to Dela. "I couldn't believe I'd heard right. When I asked him about the comment, all he said was 'what do you think I'm going to do?'"

She wiped at the tears trickling down her cheeks. "I said I thought he was for the breaching, but now, I wasn't sure." Stacy rubbed her hands up and down her arms. "He looked as if I'd slapped him."

Stacy slid her gaze back and forth between Dela and Quinn. "It was Kevin's idea to do these summits. To see how much support he could get for the breaching." She glanced at the older couple in the room. "I came along to spend time with Melba and Butch."

Tears streamed down the woman's face. "H-how did he die?"

Dela glanced at Quinn. She wasn't sure how much should be told.

"It's a homicide," Quinn said.

The woman stared at him. "Homicide? That means…someone deliberately killed him?"

"What did you think he died of?" Dela asked.

She shook her head. "I don't know. I didn't expect someone had killed him. You hear of young CEOs and VPs having heart attacks and such from stress. I-I guess I thought it was health-related." Stacy put her face in her hands and wept.

"I'm sorry to have to ask you this, but what time did you leave the casino?" Quinn asked.

The woman sniffed, wiped at her tears, and stared at him. "It was close to one?" She flicked a glance at Ben.

"Yeah. She called grandma after midnight. I drove as fast as I could because grandma said Stacy sounded upset." Ben had released the woman's shoulders but remained close.

"Was your husband in the room when you left?" Quinn asked.

"He'd followed me back to the room. He questioned how I could think he'd hurt my family. I told him the conversation I'd overheard, and he got this look in his eyes. It scared me." She glanced down at her hands and then back up at Dela.

"When he left the room, I called Melba, packed up one set of clothes and my toiletries, and waited out in the parking lot for Ben. I didn't want to meet up with Kevin again until he'd simmered down. I figured he'd come to get me this evening after the day's seminars." Tears flooded her brown eyes and trickled down her cheeks. "But now he isn't coming, is he?"

Chapter Three

They sat in the SUV outside of the Rose home. "She looked genuinely torn up," Quinn said.

Dela nodded. "I don't think she killed her husband. But did you notice how quick Ben was to comfort her?"

"They are family," Quinn said, backing the vehicle and turning around.

"Maybe." Dela didn't have any family that she knew of other than her mom. Even if she'd had cousins, she wouldn't have wanted one hanging on her like Ben had been hanging on Stacy. It felt creepy to Dela. She planned to give Stacy time to get used to the idea her husband wasn't coming home before she asked about the woman's relationship with Ben.

Quinn drove Dela back to the casino. "Is the summit still going?"

"It has two more days. I already had Bruce detain the attendees when they arrived for a presentation this morning." Dela had known they needed to question everyone involved in the summit.

"Good. We can start questioning them as soon as we get back."

That seemed to be the end of the conversation. Dela was good with that. For some reason seeing Heath had her insides stirred up. He'd known all her fears and nightmares when they were in high school. She had a feeling he could deal with her missing lower limb better than the man sitting next to her.

"How does Mugshot like the new place?" Quinn asked.

She shook her head, dispersing the thoughts that had slipped into her usually logical brain. "He likes it. The yard is large enough he can run around throwing a rope or toys in the air. The doghouse Travis built for him will keep him warm in the winter and cool in the summer. I'd never heard of putting insulation in a doghouse before, but Travis insisted that if Mugshot would be spending all the time I'm working outside, he would need a state-of-the-art home." She laughed. Travis had made a whole presentation when he gave her his proposal for the doghouse.

"Maybe I need to visit Mugshot's house since you don't want me in yours." His tone no longer held hurt. Quinn had said the words as if joking, but his wrinkled brow and twitching jaw said he wasn't.

"I have one chair. I haven't had time to furnish the rooms or do any decorating. In fact, Travis is still remodeling the bedroom and workout room. I've been sleeping in the recliner in the living room." She wanted him to see that she wasn't ready for company. Especially his.

"Do you have a table and chairs? I could bring

pizza over."

"I have a small card table and one chair. When the house is finished and I see what funds I have left for furniture, then I'll get some." She was relieved when they pulled into the casino parking lot.

Quinn parked close to the entrance. He'd discovered her limp, but as far as she knew, he hadn't learned about her missing lower limb. That was something none of her friends, or co-workers who knew, would ever tell him. It was her story to tell and they all understood that.

Now her mother…She didn't have Native American etiquette even though she'd taught school on the reservation for over thirty years. Keeping Quinn and her mom apart would be easier now that Dela no longer lived at home.

"Let's head straight to the conference area and start questioning the attendees," she said, pushing through the first set of doors before Quinn. The second set opened automatically. The sound of electronic music, dinging, and voices hung in the air along with the acrid scent of cigarette smoke. The Thursday morning buses from the senior centers in NE Oregon had arrived. One Thursday a month was Senior Day. Busloads of senior citizens arrived for a day of playing the slots, half-priced menus, and a special Bingo tournament. They would all be gone by six tonight.

The banks of slot machines had groups of men and women aged sixty and up crowded around waiting for the Bingo Tournament to start.

"Want to grab some lunch before we start questioning?" Quinn asked, walking to the left towards the Coffee Shop.

"Not really. I'm pretty sure Detective Dick has already started questioning people. He doesn't know the right question to ask." Dela continued across the casino floor to the event center.

One of her staff was standing guard at the entrance. "Ross, what are you doing here?"

"Detective Jones told me to stand here and make sure no one goes out." He raised his eyebrows. "You weren't around to tell him otherwise."

"It's probably a good idea to keep everyone with the summit inside so we can question them. Do you know what questions he's asking?" She didn't want to look like an idiot by asking the same one.

"Not a clue. I've been out here. He has a tribal with him."

"Thanks." She continued to the largest auditorium room. Everyone was seated with Tribal Officer Jacob Red Bear standing near a door to a smaller room.

Dela strode over to him, a smile on her face. Jacob was the brother of her best friend in high school. They had bonded over the loss of his sister. Dela would give both her legs to have made her friend ride home with her that day. Instead, Dela had driven off to attend basketball practice and left her friend to be picked up by someone who had raped and killed her. Her smile dimmed, as the last conversation with her friend played in her mind as it had so many times over the years. It was after that incident that she and Heath had drifted apart. It took Dela years to forgive herself, but she still couldn't shake all the blame she felt.

"Hey. I figured you'd be here asking questions before now," Jacob said.

"Special Agent Pierce and I talked to the wife

first."

He nodded. "Half the homicides are caused by the spouse. Learn anything?"

"Not that I'm at liberty to say right now. Any idea what Detective D-Jones is asking?"

Jacob snickered at her almost slip of the man's name. "He's mainly asking if anyone knew what the two were fighting about."

Dela nodded. Good. She could ask anything but that and not look like she wasn't included in the tribal police's investigation.

There were forty people sitting in the seats. "Is this everyone who came to the summit?"

"Other than the guy in the room with Detective Jones right now."

"There were two other speakers. Where are they?" She scanned the room, trying to remember the photos on the brochure she'd picked up last night.

"One is over there, and the other is here." Jacob pointed to opposite sides of the room. "They are on opposing sides of the conversation."

Dela grinned. "I see. Well, I'm going to ask them all one question. From their answers, I'll take people over at that corner of the room."

Jacob nodded.

Walking to the front of the room, Dela stopped in front of the podium. "I'm sorry the summit has been detained for the day." She went on to say who she was and that she was working with the FBI and Tribal Police to help discover what had happened to Mr. Silva.

"Is it true his wife killed him?" a man in the back of the group shouted.

Voices murmured as Dela shook her head.

"I spoke with his wife this morning. She is in shock. As you all saw, they had an argument last night in the casino. After which, she had a family member pick her up. That is where she has been staying. At this time, she isn't a person of interest."

Quinn walked in the room, his hands holding a cup carrier and what looked like two sandwiches. As he walked down the aisle to the front of the room, Dela continued.

"I would like to know how many of you talked to Mr. Silva yesterday after the seminars ended? A show of hands will be sufficient."

Eight people raised their hands.

She smiled. "I'd like you eight to move to the lower right corner of the room please." The six men and two women rose from their seats and moved to the area she'd requested.

"What are you doing?" Quinn asked, stopping beside her.

"Whittling down the number of people we need to talk with." She smiled at the group. "Now a show of hands of the people who are against breaching the dams."

About a third, including half of the people who she had already moved to the corner of the room.

"Good. Will all those against breaching move to the right of the auditorium and all those for, to the left. Thank you. We'll get to you as quickly as we can." She walked over to Jacob. "Can you ask the person Detective D-Jones is talking with the same questions when they come out and direct him or her to the area they best fit?"

"I can do that. But it's taken the detective several

hours to only talk to a quarter of the people. I can start asking questions if you tell me what to ask." Jacob was going to make a good detective one day. She was sure of that.

"Will it get you in trouble with Detective Dick?" She didn't use the correct name this time to remind her friend who he was dealing with.

"Not if I share what I learn with him."

"Okay. Ask them what they thought of Mr. Silva, and if they saw him arguing with anyone other than his wife."

"That's easy enough. I'll start on this side."

She nodded and walked over to where Quinn had set up a small table with two chairs on one side and one on the other. Dela plucked one of the sandwiches off the drinks and opened it as Quinn called down their first person and asked, "Name and occupation?"

"Jerry Timmons, Biologist with the Idaho Fish and Wildlife. I was to speak today on the need for breaching the dams. Any chance I'll get to give my speech?"

Dela ate her sandwich, letting Quinn answer. She did, however, keep her gaze on the man to see his reactions. Watching a person could tell you as much as what they said.

"Once we talk to everyone, the summit can go back to normal. Well, as normal as it can with one of your speakers having been murdered." Quinn studied the man.

Timmons blinked several times. "Living on a reservation, I've seen death. But never to someone like Kevin. He was a good guy. Even though his paycheck came from the power company, he wanted to do what would be best for the fish."

"You knew him before this summit?" Quinn asked.

"Yeah. We've been talking for years. His position kept him in contact with all the fish and wildlife biologists and the fish hatcheries. He was the liaison between the power company and those that want to protect the fish." The man shook his head. "I never thought having a summit would bring out so much animosity."

"What do you mean?" Dela asked, scrunching up the sandwich wrapper and leaning forward.

"Before Kevin started talking yesterday, he had two people in his face wanting to know how he could let fish ruin so many family's livelihoods."

"Which two?" Quinn asked.

"Some woman, I've never seen before, and Harvey Beecher. He's a farmer who will have half of his farm underwater when the dams are breached. He has been against this since the beginning of talks."

"Can you point them out?" Dela asked, scanning the people sitting in the room.

"That's Harvey up there. Sitting all by himself." Timmons pointed to a tall thin man in the back of the section with the people opposed to the breaching.

Timmons' gaze skimmed over the rest of the group. "I don't see the woman."

"Did anyone else argue with Mr. Silva?" Quinn asked. "Say later in the evening, after the meetings?"

"No. I don't believe I saw anyone, other than his wife, arguing with him."

"Where were you around midnight?" Dela asked. They didn't have a true time of death yet, but she was pretty sure the killing happened after Stacy Silva left the casino. She'd said her husband stormed out of the room. He had to have someone in mind he was going to talk with when he left the room angrily.

"Midnight? I played some cards, a couple slots, and had a nightcap in the bar and grill. Then I went up to bed. I think the clock said it was one-thirty or thereabout." Timmons had closed his eyes toward the end of the sentence. He was either trying to envision the clock or he was hiding his lie.

"Thank you. You'll need to remain unless you've already spoken with Detective Jones," Quinn said.

"I did talk to him earlier. He told me I had to stick around in case he had more questions, though."

Dela glanced at Quinn. Did they dare override Detective Dick's order?

"Then I guess you'd better hang around," Quinn said.

They didn't want to get on the tribal police detective's bad side. If it were any other lead on the tribal police, they would have all three been sitting side by side working the case together. But Dick liked to think he was smarter than them. To him, it was a contest of who found the killer first. That wasn't a good way to go about trying to solve a homicide.

They called down the next person. Quinn asked for his name and occupation.

"Tommy Darkhorse. I'm the advocate for the Columbia River Tribes. I was sent here to learn what I can and see how we can help to prove the breaching of the dams will help our native foods."

"How did you feel about Kevin Silva?" Dela asked.

"He is a good speaker. He makes you believe the power company is looking toward the interests of the fish, but I'm not sure that is true."

Quinn jumped in. "Why do you think that?"

"He talked a good talk yesterday. Then I saw him sitting in the bar with two people who have a lot to gain by not helping the fish. When I asked him about it, he said he was just listening to all sides. But then, this lady told me he wasn't even leaning toward the fish. He was going to get a bonus from the power company if he kept the dams in place." The man's face darkened in color and his facial muscles tightened as he talked about the fact Silva may have been playing them all.

Dela studied the man. Could Silva have also been playing his wife, and she'd decided she'd had enough?

Chapter Four

"What is the woman's name?" Dela asked.

Tommy Darkhorse shrugged. "Some lady who was sitting next to the table where Silva was talking with the other power people."

"Is she in this room?" Quinn asked.

Darkhorse scanned the room. "I don't see her."

"Do you remember if she was at the seminars yesterday?" Quinn asked.

"I'm not sure. She came up to me in the bar and sat down. That's when she told me what she'd overheard. I was furious. Kevin had been talking to me earlier in the day. He'd asked good questions and agreed with things I said. I really thought he was for the fish. After talking to that woman, I think he talks with two faces."

"Did you try to ask him about his change of mind last night? After you talked to the woman?" Dela asked.

"I couldn't find him down here in the casino. I asked what his room number was and no one would tell me. So, I went to bed. Figured I could corner him this morning."

Dela wondered if the man really gave up that easily. "Did you look for him this morning before the seminars started?"

"Yeah. I never saw him and then I heard he was dead." The man clamped his mouth shut.

That was all they'd get from him. For now.

"Thank you, Mr. Darkhorse. You'll have to remain until the tribal police say you may go." Quinn waited for the man to walk away. "What do you think?"

"I'm wondering if Tommy's woman is the same woman that Timmons saw arguing with Silva yesterday before the seminars started?" Dela pulled out her phone and texted Marty Casper in surveillance. *Can you put together surveillance of the bar and grill last night from the end of the seminars at the Save Our Fish Summit until it closed?*

In less than a minute, and the time Quinn asked another person to the table, her phone vibrated.

Yes.

Thanks.

Dela tipped her phone toward Quinn to see. He nodded.

They continued to question the remaining people for breaching the dam until Detective Dick stepped into the auditorium and spotted them. He frowned and stalked toward them.

"I've been questioning people. You don't need to do it, too," he said, pointing at the notebook where Quinn had been writing down people's names and information.

"We're just trying to help get the information

faster," Quinn said. "I'll type up my FD three-zero-two tonight and send you a copy. It would be courteous if you would do the same with the information you've gathered."

The detective narrowed his eyes and glared first at Quinn, then at Dela. "Did you tell him to butt in?"

Dela raised her hands. "Your MDI told me he called the FBI. Which is as it should be. I'm just sitting in to see if security or surveillance can be of help to the investigation."

Detective Dick made a noise in his throat. She wasn't sure if it was disgust or him choking on how she'd made it sound like she didn't have a care about the outcome of the investigation. In fact, she had a very palpable need to know who killed the main speaker of the Save Our Fish Summit being held at the casino. She had no doubt a phone call would be coming soon from Bernie Moon, the casino's chairman of the board of trustees, asking her if she had this situation contained. Meaning, no publicity.

Dick swung his gaze back to Quinn. "Have you found anyone of interest?"

Quinn tapped his notebook. "Not that I can tell yet. We need to verify a couple of the comments that were made about the victim."

"I see." Detective Dick smiled. "I finished with the group on that side of the room. I'll drop my notes off at the station and have them typed up. You can pick them up when you drop off your notes. I'm going to call the victim's wife. I heard she left last night after the fight in the casino."

Dela glanced at Quinn, willing him not to say anything. She knew the FBI and Tribal Police worked closely together and that was what they needed to do, but it bunched her boyshort panties to tell Detective Dick too much. He was brash enough to talk to the wrong person about crucial information that could put the killer in motion, hiding his or her tracks better.

"We," Quinn tipped his head toward Dela, "talked to her this morning. She's staying with relatives on the reservation. You can drive up to Wildhorse Mountain if you want, but I'll have those notes typed up and on your desk in the morning."

She deflated like a slow leak in an air mattress with each word Quinn uttered telling the detective what they'd learned about the woman's whereabouts.

Dick glanced at Dela, then nodded his head. "I'll go see if the forensic team is finished in the room." The man walked in front of the stage, up the aisle, and out of the auditorium.

Dela settled back in the chair. "How did you know he wouldn't decide to go talk to Stacy Silva himself?"

Quinn tapped his watch. "It's four. He wouldn't want to work past five."

Dela snickered. "We might as well let the rest of these people leave." She waved a hand to the dozen people who had been waiting to talk with the detective.

"There's no reason to keep them." Quinn stood. "You may all go back to your rooms or enjoy the casino. But please don't go home. You'll have two days of seminars to get packed into tomorrow."

Standing, Dela whispered, "That was a sneaky way of making sure they stick around without letting them know they are all still suspects."

Quinn grinned. "I have lots of evasive tactics."

This toppled her mirth. "Yes, I've seen them used

before." The memory of him outranking her and using the phrase "the U.S.'s best interest" that had taken a rapist out of her jail and set him free, came racing back along with the anger. That had been hard to swallow back in Iraq, and it still raised her hackles seven years later.

She wasn't sure if Quinn ignored her jab or didn't hear it. He was striding over to Jacob. Dela picked up the pace to hear what Jacob had learned.

"Two people said they saw Mr. Silva in a heated discussion with a blonde woman who wasn't his wife earlier in the evening," Jacob said.

"They didn't know the woman's name?" Dela asked, stopping beside Quinn.

"No. One thought they saw her at the last summit. The other didn't have any idea if they'd seen her before or not."

"Did they say where this discussion took place?" Quinn asked.

"Yeah, in the bar and grill," Jacob answered. "Another person saw an Indigenous man poking a finger in the victim's chest as they talked. This was in the lobby near the elevators. And another person said a Mr. Beecher was red in the face and spitting as he talked to the victim outside of the auditorium yesterday at the close of the seminars for the day."

"Good information," Dela said, smiling at the tribal policeman. She faced Quinn. "Sounds like we have more to check out in the security footage."

They made their way out of the auditorium and along the wall to the secret door that hid the surveillance headquarters.

Dela tapped her security clearance card against the

square box on the wall and a door opened. She and Quinn stepped through and the door closed behind them. The large room had monitors covering both the side walls. Four employees sat in front of the banks of monitors watching for unusual activity.

"Hey, Dela. Heard we had another murder," Lionel, one of the oldest security and surveillance members, said, before returning his attention to his screens.

"Yeah, not a good thing for the casino. Did any of you happen to see Mr. Silva, the victim, in any altercations yesterday on your shift?" Quinn asked.

The four surveillance employees all kept their attention on the monitors as if Quinn hadn't asked.

Dela hid the smile that twitched her lips. Three of the four employees were Umatilla members. The other one was married to a Umatilla man. Indigenous people stick together and still have an aversion to helping anyone they consider to be the government. FBI Special Agent Pierce was considered the enemy, even though he'd walked in the room with her.

She wasn't Indigenous but having grown up on the reservation while her mom taught at the reservation grade school, she was considered one of them.

"Did you see Mr. Silva in any arguments other than the one he had on the casino floor with his wife last night?" Dela asked.

Maureen, the wife of a Umatilla member, nodded. "He had words with a blonde-haired woman outside of the event center around eleven in the morning. I also saw them later in the bar and grill sharing a table."

"After they had the argument?" Dela asked, stepping up alongside Maureen's chair.

"Yeah, a couple of hours later. Around one? I think it was the events lunch break." The woman tipped her head back to peer into Dela's face. "They looked chummy then."

Dela glanced at Quinn. Who was this mystery blonde?

Chapter Five

Dela had her prosthetic foot up on the box under the head of surveillance's table. Marty kept the box there for her to prop her foot on when she went over surveillance tapes with him. He, and the last Head of Security, were the only two people at the casino who had witnessed Dela in pain at work. Since that one time, she tried to not work so many hours that her stub became sore and inflamed. Unfortunately, at times like this, she put in longer hours.

"We know that the woman we are trying to find out about was in the bar and grill with our victim last night. Can you pull up the feed from the Pony Bar?" she asked.

"I queued it up after you sent the text. Do you want me to go to a specific time?" Marty held his hands over the keyboard.

Dela glanced at Quinn. "Want to go straight to the woman talking to the victim or watch how the evening

43

plays out?"

"Let's start at when the victim enters the bar and grill the first time."

Marty started tapping keys. The video started, but he fast-forwarded until Mr. Silva walked into the Pony Grill. The victim and the other two speakers sat at a table together. After they ordered drinks, the conversation appeared to become heated.

"Do you think they are this riled up over the topic of the summit?" Dela asked.

"It's a pretty hot topic," Marty said.

"There, see that woman slip out of the chair where she is and walk over to Darkhorse?" Quinn pointed to a blonde woman wearing a dress that said, look at me. It clung to her body, cut low in the front, and barely covered her ass.

"That's a summit attendee?" Dela thought the woman looked more like a high-class hooker.

"I'm surprised that man can keep his eyes on her face," Marty said.

Dela glared at the head of surveillance.

"What? I'm just saying. I bet FBI man wouldn't have noticed her getting up if she hadn't been dressed like eye candy."

She shot a glance at Quinn. He was studying the monitor with avid interest. Was it to see the woman's cleavage or to see the expressions on her face and Tommy's?

The other two men at Mr. Silva's table rose and walked out. The victim ran a hand through his hair and pulled out his phone. He texted, waited, smiled, and tossed money on the table before leaving. Whoever he texted had made his evening better.

The victim had barely disappeared through the door and Tommy Darkhorse shot out of his chair.

"Follow him," Quinn said.

Marty tapped keys on the keyboard and an image of the casino popped on the screen. Tommy was following the victim. Near the elevator, Tommy must have called out the victim's name. Silva turned and the Indigenous man was in his face. Poking the victim in the chest with his finger. His face grew darker as his mouth moved, saying something that had Silva backing up with his hands in the air.

"If there was a gun, I'd say that was a robbery," Marty said.

"Darkhorse is definitely angry with the victim over something." Quinn wrote down the time in his notebook.

Mr. Silva said something that seemed to switch Tommy's attitude. They shook hands. Mr. Silva entered the elevator, and Tommy walked away.

"Can you bring up the footage outside the auditorium yesterday after the seminars ended?" Quinn asked.

"It'll take a few minutes."

"Before you do that, can you print a photo of the woman's face?" Dela asked. "I want to see if anyone in registration knows who she is."

"Good idea," Quinn said.

"I have one now and then," she quipped, as Marty stopped the video on a section with a good look at the woman's face. He put a box around the face and the printer began to whir.

"I'll get the other footage up." His fingers flashed on the keyboard and video of the area in front of the event center appeared on the monitor.

"Do you have a time?" Marty asked.

"Not really." Dela shrugged.

He backed it up to 3 pm. "What am I looking for?"

"A man got in the victim's face according to witnesses. I'd like to see the confrontation." Quinn leaned forward in his chair. "There. That's the man."

Marty slowed the video. They watched as Mr. Beecher stopped in front of Mr. Silva, not allowing him to step around, and shouted at him.

Dela made a face watching as the angry man's spittle, did indeed, fly in the direction of Mr. Silva. The victim didn't flinch or wipe his face. She wouldn't have been able to stay that calm with someone screaming and spitting in her face. She'd barely held it together when her drill sergeant yelled at her in boot camp. It appeared Mr. Silva was the right person to be handling the topic of the Save Our Fish Summit.

"We need to talk to that man." Quinn stood.

"What about seeing how cozy the woman was with the victim later last night?" Dela was more interested in the woman who seemed to be trying to cause trouble.

Quinn sat back down. "Sure. But that man there," he pointed to Beecher, "he has anger issues."

"I don't disagree. But as long as we are here, let's look at all the video we can." Dela shifted her foot on the box. "Marty, can you bring up the Pony Grill a little before one, please."

The head of surveillance had the screen filled with the Pony Grill after a few taps on the keyboard.

They watched as the victim ambled in and sat down at the bar. It was apparent he didn't have plans to hook up with anyone. He was most likely drinking away the fact his wife didn't believe him.

The bleached blonde walked in, scanned the room, and went straight to the victim. She put a hand on his shoulder and pressed her D-cup breast against his arm. Definitely trying to make their meeting look intimate. But why?

Mr. Silva leaned away, looked at her, and a weak smile formed on his lips.

She sat down next to him, keeping her body leaning in his direction. It was evident she was doing all the seducing. Their backs were to the camera.

"Damn, I wish I could see their faces." Frustrated, she shoved her chair back and stood. Her knee had stiffened a bit while sitting. She didn't like Quinn to see how her handicap affected her. As if Marty understood, he jumped up and grabbed the photo out of the printer, handing it to her.

"Thank you." She nodded to the door. "Let's go get a name for this woman."

Quinn headed to the door. She mouthed, thank you, to Marty as she swung her right leg back and forth, making the joint loosen up before she walked across the room and followed Quinn out into the larger room.

In the casino, Senior Bingo was in full swing. Less people filled the slot machine islands. However, the noise of voices from the Bingo room drowned out the usual flute music that piped through the establishment.

The lines at the registration desk were three deep. Dela sighed, spun, and smiled. Rosie waved at her from the deli.

"Let's get something to drink," Dela said, heading for the deli counter. Rosie was a welcome sight. She paid attention to everyone she saw and had a mind for remembering names, faces, and anything people told her.

"Hi, Handsome," Rosie greeted Quinn, wiggling her eyebrows. "When you going to come here by yourself so we can get to know one another better?"

"Rosie, I tend to only come here when there is trouble. Which doesn't give me time to flirt with you." He stepped closer to the counter. "But I'll have to make it a date to come by some time when I'm not working."

The woman giggled and winked at Dela. "I like him. If you don't grab him up, I will."

Dela waved her hand. "You can have him."

Rosie nodded her head. "Sure, now I heard Heath Seaver is back. You and him going to pick up where you left off?"

Her insides twisted. Dela forgot Rosie was only a few years older than she and Heath and, with her memory, would remember who dated who. "We parted as friends and will remain, just friends."

"I thought you said you two just went to school together?" Quinn asked, staring her in the eyes.

"And all the dances, football games, and school events," Rosie added.

Dela slapped the photo of the woman on the counter in front of Rosie. "Have you seen this woman? Any chance you know if she's staying in the hotel?" She couldn't ignore the hurt in Rosie's eyes. "I'm sorry. Trying to get settled in my new place, this homicide, and you bringing up times before… Well, I'd like to just stick to finding out who killed the Save Our Fish Summit's main speaker."

The woman nodded. Her eyes softened. "No one blames you for Robin's death. Only you."

Quinn took a step closer to Dela. "Who is Robin?"

"No one you should be interested in." Dela straightened her back and forced her lips into a smile. "Rosie, have you seen this woman?"

"Yes. She sat over at that table on a computer and her phone during most of yesterday." The woman pointed to a table at the back of the eating area.

"Did she order food and give a name?" Dela asked.

"Connie was the name she gave for her food orders. But she also used a card to purchase the food. It said Constance Oswood." Rosie smiled and her eyes lit up. Her memory was a superpower.

"Thanks, Rosie! Now we know who to look for. I'll have a lemonade and…" she glanced at Quinn, "Did you want something to drink?"

"Coffee. Black."

Rosie spun around to the drink dispenser behind her and began filling cups.

"You going to tell me about this Robin person?" Quinn asked quietly.

"Maybe someday. I'm still not ready to let it go." Her chest squeezed. She and Robin had been more like sisters than friends. They'd spent weekends at one another's home, went to all the school events together, even when she was dating Heath. He didn't mind that Robin came along and would sometimes invite one of his friends.

"Here you go." Rosie held out their drinks. "I hope you get this solved before all the people here for the summit go home."

"I doubt we can solve it that quickly, but that would be ideal." Quinn paid for their drinks.

Dela headed to the registration desk. Now that they

had a name, she could look up the guest herself. She nodded to her friend, Faith Whitebird, who was registering a guest and walked over to an unmanned computer.

Quinn leaned on the other side of the counter as she typed in the name Constance Oswood.

The room and her billing information popped up. "Will you look at that?" Dela wrote down the room number and the company that was paying for the room.

"What?" Quinn leaned more, trying to see the screen.

"Ms. Oswood's room is being paid for by a larger power company than Hells Canyon Power." She turned off the screen and walked back to the gate that kept non-employees out from behind the counter.

"That's interesting." Quinn grasped her hand holding the paper with the information. He read it and released her. "I think we need to have a talk with Ms. Oswood."

Using the phone at the registration desk, Dela called room 1016. No one answered.

"She's not in the room." She glanced at her watch. "She's either eating dinner or having a drink before dinner. Let's save some leg work." She pulled out her cell phone and dialed Marty.

"Yo, did you find out who the woman is?" he answered.

"Yes, and she's not in her room. Any chance you can walk out and check the monitors and let me know if she's in the casino?"

"Call you back in a few."

Silence.

"Marty's looking on the surveillance monitors to

see where she is." Dela leaned against the registration counter.

"You two loiterers have a reason for leaning on my counter?" Faith asked, smiling and stopping next to Dela.

"We're waiting for Marty to call us back," Dela said. She held up the photo of Connie Oswood. "Know anything about this woman?"

Faith grasped the paper and stared at it. "Yeah, she likes to use her body to get what she wants." She shoved the paper back at Dela.

"And you know this how?" Quinn asked.

"By looking at her and seeing what she wears. A woman who dresses like her, uses their body to get what they want as much as they use their brains." Faith put a hand on one hip. "Don't tell me the big bad FBI man hadn't noticed her attributes."

Dela noticed Quinn's face grew a tad redder. He had noticed the woman's attributes. "Have you seen her with anyone in particular?"

Faith shook her head. "Always alone."

Dela's phone buzzed. Marty. "Where is she?"

"The Pony Grill. She's at a table with one of the men you were interested in earlier. The one who was spitting mad."

"Thanks." Dela shoved her phone in her pocket. "Come on. She's in the grill with Beecher." She was going to let Quinn tackle questioning the man.

Chapter Six

Stepping into the Pony Grill, Dela's gaze quickly found Ms. Oswood and Mr. Beecher. They were an unlikely looking couple. The woman was in another tight-fitting dress, that showed off more of her body than Dela showed off when she went swimming. The man was in overalls and a checkered flannel shirt.

Quinn approached the table, holding out his hand. "Ms. Oswood, we haven't met. I'm Special Agent Quinn Pierce with the FBI and this is Dela Alvaro, head of security for the casino." Quinn took the chair to the right of the woman and nodded to the seat across from him.

Dela sent him a brief glare and walked around to the other side of the table.

"Why do you want to talk to Connie?" Mr. Beecher asked.

"Because she wasn't in the auditorium earlier today

when we interviewed all the summit attendees," Quinn said, directing his attention to the man.

"You didn't talk to me," he said.

"No. But you were interviewed by Detective Jones of the Tribal Police. We are working together to discover who killed Mr. Silva." Quinn studied Mr. Beecher.

Dela flicked her gaze from one face to the other. The farmer appeared more nervous than the woman.

"Damn shame that happened," Mr. Beecher said, without a single ounce of sincerity.

"He was an intelligent man. One who could see both sides of a situation." Ms. Oswood at least sounded upset.

Quinn swung his gaze to the woman. "When was the last time you saw Mr. Silva yesterday?"

"Around one a.m. Here. He was having a nightcap, and I came in and found him all alone. I asked where his pretty wife was. He said she had a headache from all the smoke and noise."

Dela glanced at Quinn. He had drawn his notepad out and was taking notes. According to the deceased's wife, she left before he went to the bar and grill. Who was lying?

"How did you know Mr. and Mrs. Silva?" Quinn asked.

"I met Mr. Silva at one of the other conferences held in Idaho and Mrs. Silva at this one. I checked in at the same time on Wednesday morning." Ms. Oswood picked up her drink, keeping eye contact with Quinn.

Dela decided she needed to take charge of the conversation since she was immune to the woman's flirting. "Why are you at this summit, Ms. Oswood?"

"Call me Connie. Anyone is invited." She slowly drew her gaze from Quinn's and smiled at Dela.

"Yes, but you said you'd met Mr. Silva at another summit. How many have you attended?" She wanted to ask, 'are you so slow you need to hear the information multiple times,' but she knew that wasn't the reason. And she didn't want to get kicked off the investigation for being bitchy.

The woman shrugged. "I've been to all that have been put on so far. I'm a reporter. It's my job to report what happens and who is for or against the breaching."

A quick glance at Quinn held Dela's tongue. They knew her room had been paid for by a power company. If she was a reporter, there was only one side she was reporting.

"I see. What paper do you write for?" Quinn asked.

"A small one you probably haven't heard of." She smiled and licked her top lip.

Dela rolled her eyes at the woman's not-so-subtle attempt at flirtation.

"I've worked all over the Pacific Northwest, I'm sure I've heard of it." Quinn had his hand poised over the notepad in front of him.

Mr. Beecher cleared his throat.

Dela shot a glance his direction. He was trying to deflect them from the woman. He knew she wasn't really a reporter.

"Do you have something to say, Mr. Beecher? Like you know this woman is lying. She isn't a reporter, is she?" Dela was tired of this roundabout way Quinn had been questioning. The woman sent the hair on the back of her neck tingling. It was how she'd felt in Iraq when they were out on patrol right before they'd be under direct fire.

"I barely know her. How would I know if she's lying or not?" The man's face turned bright red as his voice grew louder.

"You bonded over the fact you both don't want the dams to be breached?" Dela continued, ignoring Quinn's head shake and frown. "I bet this is a congratulatory drink that your main problem, Mr. Silva, is no longer a problem."

"Dela," Quinn said in a low growl.

She glared back at him.

Ms. Oswood put a hand on Quinn's arm. "She's fine. I get this all the time from women who feel threatened by me."

Dela had some choice words, but instead, sent a steely glare at the woman. "I'm not threatened by you, Ms. Oswood. But I, being a woman, can see you have made your way in this world by influencing men with your body, while I've managed to survive a war and this reservation by using my wits. I'm just making sure my colleague and Mr. Beecher realize they are being manipulated by your cunning and their testosterone." She smiled sweetly at the woman whose eyes widened before narrowing.

"We saw the video of you trying to seduce Mr. Silva last night, right here, in this bar. You just said you knew he had a wife. Were you trying to get some dirt on him to get him to back off on breaching the dams, or were you trying to get an invitation to his room so you could kill him?"

Dela shot a quick glance at Quinn, he was staring at the woman.

"Dela asked you a question," he said to Ms.

Oswood.

The woman's eyes softened as she shifted her gaze to Quinn. "I was merely looking for entertainment last night. When he said he had to get back to his wife and left, I took that as my sign to take myself up to my own lonely bed." She put a hand on Quinn's arm again. "Now, if you wanted to keep me company tonight, I wouldn't turn you down."

Dela about gagged on the woman's actions and words. She spun her gaze to Mr. Beecher. He didn't appear jealous, but his face had darkened like a beet and his hands gripped his glass hard enough his knuckles were white. Did he have a thing for the woman or was he worried she would give something away?

"When was the last time you saw Mr. Silva?" Dela asked the farmer.

He picked up his glass and drank the beer. Setting the glass on the table he stood. "After the summit yesterday. Never did see him again." Without another word, he walked out of the bar.

"And now I'm down to one." Ms. Oswood walked her fingers up Quinn's arm. "Would you escort me to my room? I wouldn't want to become the next victim you are investigating."

Dela stood. "Go ahead. I'm heading home."

She walked out of the bar and grill. She knew that Quinn wouldn't jeopardize the case by getting mixed up with one of the suspects. But she wanted to give him room to maybe get more out of the woman if she thought he might take her up on her invitation.

The night valet, Albert, was on duty. He was the male equivalent of Rosie. He never forgot a face, a name, or how many times the person had visited the casino.

"Dela, what are you doing here so early on a Thursday night?" Albert asked as she walked up to him.

"I've been here all day."

The man nodded. "The murder last night. I heard about it from a nephew this afternoon. They say it was one of the summit people."

"It was. The main speaker, Kevin Silva. Do you remember seeing him or his wife?" She pulled a chair from the nearest slot machine over and sat next to Albert so he could watch the casino floor and keep an eye outside for any cars pulling up to valet parking.

"He was a nice man. I saw the argument at the blackjack table and watched his wife get in the elevator." He shook his head. "I also saw her leave with a younger man around one. I was out getting a car for someone and saw her get into an older model Camaro. I'm pretty sure it belongs to Butch Rose. But his grandson drives it these days."

Dela nodded. "Yes. Mrs. Silva and Ben both said he picked her up after she'd called the Rose house asking for someone to come get her. They are relatives."

"That would explain young Ben picking her up. But why did she leave? Because of the argument?" Albert studied her for a few seconds before casting his gaze toward the parking lot and then the casino floor.

"Yes. She wanted to clear her head. Her husband had told her one thing and other people were telling her something different."

"It's a sad thing when married people don't trust one another." His eyes stared at the water feature toward the back of the casino near the lobby. "Even when it was arranged marriages and the couples didn't love each other, they at least respected and trusted one another. It was necessary to survive."

Grandfather Thunder had told her about arranged marriages when she was a teenager. She never did figure out why he thought it was necessary to tell her about an old practice that had gone on in many cultures.

"Was that jealousy that sent you stomping away from our interview?" Quinn asked, standing in front of her with his arms crossed and his legs spread apart like some mythical god who thought he could make her speak.

"No, I was giving you room to make her think you were interested so she would open up to you."

Quinn laughed until tears glistened in his eyes. "That's you giving me room to work? You acted like some spinster who couldn't take being around a woman who knew she was sexy."

Anger spiked fast, hot, and violent. She shot up off the chair, her fist directed at his jaw. Her hit landed before she realized what she'd done or Quinn could react.

Her hand hurt, but her anger didn't lessen. "Don't ever talk to me as if I'm a woman who hates other women because of what they have and I don't have. You don't know the half of what I go through each and every day."

A hand rested gently on her shoulder. "Why don't you go home and visit with that dog I heard you have. I'm sure he'll listen better than this man." Albert propelled her out the front door.

Once she stood outside the doors, she didn't know

what to do. Her purse was in the security office with her car keys. If she stood here too long, Quinn would come out, and she didn't want to talk to him. She'd just struck an FBI agent. Granted he deserved it, but…

Dela walked around the building to the back door and let herself in with her security badge.

"Hey, I thought you were already here," Tammie said, as Dela walk stiff-legged over to her desk, pulled out her purse, and walked back to the door.

Her actions felt robotic. "I am leaving now. If Kenny has any problems, tell him to call. I'm just going home for dinner and to take care of my dog. I can come back in if he needs me." Dela didn't wait for an answer. She pushed the door open and walked to her car, wondering what the punishment was for punching an FBI agent.

Chapter Seven

At home, after petting Mugshot, giving him some dinner, and getting her prosthesis off, she sat down with her hand in a pan of water and Epsom salt. Her fingers throbbed. She hadn't punched someone in several years. While it felt good to release the frustration that had built up since losing her lower leg, she worried about getting yanked from the case and possibly losing her job for hitting a federal lawman.

Her cell phone, sitting on the end table beside the chair, buzzed. A glance at the name made her groan. Quinn.

She couldn't avoid him. Needed to hear the consequences. She picked the phone up and swiped it open.

"I'm not sorry," were her first words.

A chuckle on the phone released some of the tension in her chest. "I didn't figure you would be. I think getting hit by you was less humiliating than getting lectures from Albert and Marty. I also have text messages from Rosie, Lionel, and Kenny. It appears they are all worried about me pressing charges and you losing your job."

Knowing her casino family was behind her made her smile.

"Can I come over and discuss our strategy for tomorrow?" His wistful tone almost had her giving in.

"No. You told Detective Dick you'd have all of our interviews to him tomorrow. You need to find a computer and get typing. I want his notes."

"Sure you do. You just want an excuse to stay away from me in case you take another swing." The playfulness in his voice told her she was forgiven.

"You don't understand how women like Ms. Oswood make me feel. I was a jock growing up, then I went into the army where I was one of the guys. Your crack wasn't far off and it stung."

"Hey, I didn't mean to—"

"Forget I just said that. I'll call you in the morning when I get to the casino. Unless I get called back in tonight, at which point, I may not call until after noon." She hung up. There was no sense trying to make Quinn see that she just wanted to be seen as a woman. Something that would never happen if he knew she wasn't a whole woman.

♠ ♣ ♥ ♦

Loud barking, mixed with someone pounding on her door, woke Dela. She shushed Mugshot, eased the recliner to a sitting position, and listened.

"Dela? Come on, open the door." Heath's deep adult voice filled her with the same happiness his teenage hormone-induced voice had.

"Shit!" Her red scarred stub came into focus. "I'm not dressed," she called out.

"Get dressed! Grandfather Thunder said you hit that G-man last night. We need to talk." The doorknob rattled.

"I'm fine. Quinn called, I apologized—"

"No, you didn't. You never apologize. You better not be in there drowning your sorrows in ice cream."

She laughed, remembering how many times he'd arrived at her house to find her spooning ice cream from the carton into her mouth after a bad basketball game, a test she'd screwed up, and after Robin died.

"I'm not eating ice cream. I'm fine. Go home. You had a long day yesterday." She shoved to her foot, grasping the crutches leaning against the arm of the recliner.

Mugshot stood at the French doors, whining. She used the crutches to navigate through the living room and into the dining room to the doors. Unlocking the knob, she swung the door open. Mugshot headed out the door at the same time Dela sucked in air at the sight of Heath.

The large dog woofed and launched himself at her friend.

"Mugshot, down!" she shouted.

Heath, spread his legs, ready for the force of the one-hundred-forty-pound dog putting most of his weight on the two legs on Heath's shoulders.

"Don't hurt him," she cried, as Heath pushed the dog backward. "He only has three legs."

"Hurt him?" Heath's voice sounded winded as the dog landed on his three feet and stood between Dela and Heath, growling.

"It's okay, Mugshot, he's a friend." Dela leaned to pet the dog's back and his long, thick tail swiped away her right crutch, leaving her nothing to put her weight on. She started to topple. Both the man and the dog stopped her fall.

Her face scorched with embarrassment as Heath righted her and handed her the crutch.

"Looks like you have a lot to tell me," he said, motioning for her to move back into the house and allow him to enter.

She backed up and headed to the kitchen to start coffee. Dela needed the time to think about what to say. "Could you fill the coffeemaker?" she asked, pulling another cup out of the cupboard.

He stepped by her, filling the water tank on the single-cup coffeemaker her mom gave her as a housewarming gift.

"We don't have to talk about the fact you're on crutches right now. I'm more interested in why you hit the FBI agent and did he really forgive you?" Water splashed into the coffeemaker.

Dela held up a pod. "Do you like dark or medium roast?"

Heath leaned his butt against the counter and crossed his arms. "Medium, don't change the conversation."

She dropped a pod in the machine and hit start, before leaning against the counter across from him. "I'm not avoiding the conversation. I told you, I'm forgiven. It's not the first time Special Agent Pierce and I have had an altercation."

Heath studied her. "When did the two of you meet?"

"In Iraq, eight years ago." She didn't see any reason to hide how long she'd known Quinn.

"Iraq. That means you were stationed together in the army?"

She couldn't tell if he was just curious or didn't like that she had a history with the FBI agent. "We weren't stationed together. I was an M.P. He was special forces. They would come in and question detainees. That's how we met." She shrugged, even though there was a whole lot more to their relationship.

The coffeemaker steamed and gurgled. "Here's your cup. Sit down and I'll get dressed. But you need to know it takes me a good half an hour to get dressed."

"Sit down and have a cup of coffee with me. Then I'll leave and you can dress." His gaze drifted down to her leg.

If anyone other than Heath had stared at her stub for that long, she would have squirmed and run out of the room. She guessed because they knew each other's best and worst moments as teenagers, she didn't mind him seeing her flaws. She picked up her brewed cup of coffee and entered the living room. She set the cup on the side table and eased down onto the recliner.

Heath followed her and sat on the hearth of her dysfunctional fireplace. "Grandfather Thunder said you were discharged because of a disability. I didn't think it was anything mental. You've always been mentally strong. But I didn't realize…"

"It's okay. I don't advertise I'm a lower limb amputee. I prefer people to not know. It seems like when they find out they treat me differently." She peered into his eyes.

He nodded. "You never wanted anyone to see your

weaknesses. I get it. Who does know? I don't want to say something to the wrong person."

"Marty, the head of surveillance at the casino, Molly and Travis Taylor. She was Molly White Feather in school."

He nodded. "I heard she is a veterinarian."

Dela smiled. "I took Mugshot to her when he was hit by a teenager driving a jacked-up truck too fast. That's how I got him. The original owner didn't want to pay the vet bill or his food bill."

Heath laughed. "I bet that's more than your monthly payment on the house."

She grinned. It felt good to have someone to talk to and laugh with who she knew would never betray her.

"What have you been up to all these years?" she asked, sipping her coffee.

"Messed around a few years after high school. I ended up on a reservation in the mid-west that had poor services for the people and corrupt police services."

She studied him. "You took on the tribal government on a reservation you weren't part of?"

The gleam in his eyes dulled. "I was a part of the reservation. I finally found out who my father was."

She put a hand out. He leaned forward, taking it in his. "Did it answer the questions you had? You said 'was.' Is he no longer alive?" As she asked these questions she wondered if it was time to try and find out more about her father.

Tears glistened in Heath's eyes. He shoved a hand through his shoulder-length dark hair. "He died when I was twelve. I found an aunt and his best friend at the reservation. They filled me in on how my mom and dad met and how she refused to live in South Dakota and left without telling my father she was pregnant with me."

Dela squeezed his hand. She understood the sorrow. How many times had she wondered if her father was alive and her mother just didn't want her daughter to learn about him? "I'm so sorry. Did your aunt say he would have been happy to have known you?"

He nodded, wiped at the tears that had trickled down the side of his face. "Yes. She said if he had known, he would have found me and taken me back with him. I have two half-sisters and a half-brother at Pine Ridge. It was wonderful getting to know them. I joined the tribal police there, hoping to change things for The People." He shook his head. "When so much corruption has gone on for so long, it is like a mouse trying to move a boulder." He sighed, withdrew his hand, and leaned back. "When Grandfather Thunder told me there was an opening on the tribal police and that you were living back on the reservation, I decided it was time to come home." A weak smile barely tipped the corners of his mouth.

"I'm glad you found out the truth about your father and have discovered siblings." She stared into his eyes. "I'm glad you came back. I have never had as good a friend as you. You're what I need right now."

His smile brightened.

Her phone vibrated on the table. A glance at the name made her roll her eyes. Quinn. She picked up the phone and answered, "I said I'd call you when I arrived at the casino."

"It's after nine. When I asked security if you'd been called back in last night they said, 'no.' That made me wonder if you were avoiding me." Quinn's tone said he was irritated that she might be avoiding him.

"I'm not avoiding you. I slept late. I'll be there in an hour." She held her hand over the phone. "Did you bring back information from the autopsy?" she asked Heath in a whisper.

He frowned. "Yes. Why are you whispering?"

"Long story." She returned her attention to the phone. "I had a text from Heath. He's back with information on the autopsy. I'll have him meet us at the casino."

"Why did he text you and not me?" Quinn asked.

She sighed heavily. "Maybe because he knows I'm head of security and working with you. Did you give him your phone number?"

There was a pause. "No. But the State Examiner would have had it."

"I'm not arguing with you anymore. I'll see you in an hour." She hung up the phone and felt Heath's gaze on her.

"What?"

"Why didn't you tell whoever that was I was here?" He studied her with the same focus he'd used when they were biology partners and he was looking through the microscope.

"As you already know, my relationship—working relationship—with Special Agent Pierce is tempestuous. After all, I hit him last night." She rubbed the faint bruising on her hand.

Heath pointed a finger at her. "I think there's more to this. Are you two in a romantic relationship?"

"No! At one time, I'd thought about it. Back in Iraq. Until he undermined me and let a rapist lose."

"Why would he do that?" The indignation in Heath's voice and on his face reassured her that her anger at Quinn had been justified.

"He was special forces and insisted the man was an informant and his information was crucial in saving American lives. He felt that one man was more important than a young Iraqi woman who had lost everything, her family, her self-esteem, and ultimately her life." As she recounted the fate that had befallen the young woman, Dela's anger at Quinn rekindled.

"And here you are working with him on the rez. That has to be hard," Heath said, bringing her back to the present.

"Yeah. However, most of the time he has to let me take the lead because no one on the rez wants to talk to a Fed." She smiled. "That has helped the situation."

Heath grinned. "I bet. Puts him in his place." He stood. "I'll let you get dressed, and I'll meet you and the agent at the casino in an hour."

Dela pushed to her foot and used the crutches to stand. "I'm happy you came back. Molly and Faith are good friends, but..." She peered into his eyes. "No one else knows me like you do. It's good to have someone to talk to that I know won't judge me or try to tell me how to live."

He stepped closer, put a hand on her arm. "We know each other's fears. I think that's why I came back when Grandfather Thunder told me you'd returned. I needed that hard-headed logic only you can provide."

Warmth filled her. Finally, she had someone who understood her and could help her reconcile with herself. "You know where to find me and my hard-headed logic. You are welcome here any time." Which had her asking. "Where are you living?"

"Until I find something to rent, with my mother."

Dela couldn't stop the laughter.

"Hey, it's not that funny," Heath said, a grin on his face.

Controlling herself, she asked, "So how's that going?"

"I imagine about as well as you living with your mom went." He raised one eyebrow.

"Yeah. I hope you find something soon. As you can tell, I'm still under construction here. If you haven't found anything by the time Travis finishes with my remodel, you can rent a room from me until you find something." It would be fun having him around.

His eyes sparkled. "Rent a room?"

Her face heated. "I'm not ready to do more than be platonic with anyone of the opposite sex. I'm still figuring out who I am now that I'm missing a body part."

Heath put a hand on her cheek. "You're still the same hard-headed, infuriating, caring girl you were before. Just older, wiser, more cynical, and more filled out than that jock I used to date."

His words filled her with visions of a life she'd given up on nearly three years ago when she'd lost her foot. "I'm glad I have a few redeeming qualities. Go. I need to be at the casino in a little over thirty minutes now." She swung over to the door and held it open. "And don't tell Quinn you were here."

Heath stopped in the doorway. "Why?"

"He's been pestering me to let him come see my place. He's remodeling a Victorian house in town and wanted to see what I'm doing out here. I don't want him to see…things. I don't want him to treat me like an invalid. He knows something happened to get me medically discharged but he doesn't know about my disability."

Heath shook his head. "He's a Fed. He probably pulled up your whole medical file. I think there's a different reason you don't want him here."

"What's that?" she asked, angered that he thought he could walk into her life and in one day know what she was thinking.

"I think you and he have a love/hate relationship." Heath became serious. "Just for the record. I've known you longer and I already know he isn't right for you." With that, he spun around and strode out to his Jeep.

Chapter Eight

Quinn and Heath were sitting in the back corner booth when Dela walked into the coffee shop. Quinn had texted her to meet them here. The two men were so consumed by their conversation, they didn't see her enter. She took this time to study them.

Heath had gone home and changed into his uniform. His shoulder-length hair proved he wasn't going to let being a law enforcer take away his heritage. His shoulders weren't as broad as Quinn's but she knew he could carry a lot of weight on them. Quinn was dressed in a suit, with a light blue shirt and a contrasting tie. His light brown hair almost looked blond next to Heath's dark locks. They were both good-looking men. She sighed, stuffed her romantic thoughts down deep, and walked up to the table.

"Gentlemen, I hope I didn't keep you waiting too long."

Both their heads spun her direction. Heath's eyes

held merriment. Quinn studied her as if she'd crawled in from being hit by a truck.

"Not sure why you couldn't have been here earlier. We're wasting time." Quinn stood as if he planned on her sliding into the booth on his side.

Instead, she glanced at Heath, who slid over, allowing her to sit on the outside edge. It was easier for her to navigate sitting on the edge as opposed to having to slide across the seat to get in and back out.

"You could have continued without me. I do have a few tasks to take care of as the head of security."

Quinn frowned at her choice of seat and sat back down. He nodded toward Heath. "He refused to tell me what he'd learned at the autopsy."

Dela hid a grin. "Well, I'm here now. What did you learn?" She pivoted her head to watch her high school boyfriend as Quinn pulled his notepad out of his coat pocket.

Heath opened the folder sitting in front of him and scanned the page on top. "As you know, he was strangled with a ligature, the lamp power cord. The medical examiner ruled the death as asphyxia. She said it appeared that the victim was strangled from behind. Which means either the assailant snuck up behind him, or he didn't fear the person and had turned his back on them."

Dela cleared her throat. "Like his wife."

"Or an associate," Quinn said.

Heath nodded to both of them. "However, the Medical Examiner didn't see any signs of a struggle. No skin under his fingernails, no evidence that the victim made any attempt to fight off his attacker. Because of that, they drew blood for toxicology, but that will take a day or two for the results. There was ash on his clothing. The lab tech who took the clothing said it smelled like sage." He glanced at Dela.

"What does that mean?" Quinn asked.

"Sage is burned by our People to purify," Heath said.

"Which opens the possibility that our assailant could be Indigenous. They might have heard the victim was siding with the power company and not the fish. Went up to confront the victim, they talked, maybe Mr. Silva said something that made things seem smoothed over and then…" Dela shrugged, "for whatever reason the person snapped, strangled the victim, and then decided the man's body needed to be purified."

Quinn stood. "Let's go talk to the wife. She's Indigenous. Maybe she killed him before she left, started feeling guilty, and used the sage."

Heath frowned. "It doesn't work like that."

"No, but it doesn't hurt to talk to her again." Dela stood. "She's had time to come to grips with what happened and maybe she'll have some more information for us." She faced Quinn. "Did you get the reports from Detective Dick's interviews?"

"Detective who?" Heath asked.

Quinn grinned. "That's her pet name for Detective Jones."

"Does he know you call him that?" Heath asked. "It would make sense about why he has nothing good to say about you."

"He doesn't like me because I make him do what he's supposed to do. Help the people of this reservation." Dela wasn't going to go into the detective's shortcomings. "I just hope the rumors of his retiring are true."

She headed to the coffee shop exit.

Quinn caught up at the door. "What's your hurry?"

"I want this figured out before all of our suspects head off to their homes. It will make gathering information harder." She exited the casino and headed for Quinn's SUV.

"By the time we finish with Mrs. Silva, Shaffer should have had time to go through the victim's computer. Information in there might help the investigation."

They climbed into the vehicle and Quinn followed the same route they'd driven the day before to get to Wildhorse Mountain.

Passing Mission Market, Quinn asked, "Just how well do you and Seaver know each other?"

Dela glanced at Quinn. "I told you, we went to school together."

"And dated according to Rosie. And he seems to know an awful lot about your life since you returned to the reservation. You sure you don't want to put a restraining order on him?"

A deep belly laugh escaped before she could stop it. She laughed until tears slid down her cheeks. A swipe cleared them away, and she sobered. "Heath is not a stalker. Our families, well, Grandfather Thunder and my mom, are close. He tells her all about Heath, and she tells him all about me. I'm sure everything he knows has come from those conversations. You've met my mom. All she has to talk about are her flowers and me."

"He said your new place was coming along nice. When did you invite him over to see the house? If you didn't, then he is, indeed, a stalker." Quinn took his gaze off the road and peered at her.

She sighed. Obviously, she hadn't gotten through to Heath that she didn't want Quinn hounding her about coming to the house. "He stopped by this morning."

The vehicle was wandering toward the edge of the road. "Quinn! Look at the road, not me!"

He swerved back onto the road and stared straight ahead. "Why?"

"So we don't end up in the ditch." She fisted her hands. How could they work together if he questioned everything she did?

"No. Why did he stop by?" The low tone and the sight of his clenched jaw wasn't a good sign.

"What does it matter? We're old friends. It was nice catching up."

"Was he there when I called?" Again, his tone sounded menacing.

"Yes. I didn't say he was because I didn't want you to think…I don't know what."

The vehicle stopped at the end of the road leading up to the Rose residence. Quinn faced her. "I don't like working with people who can't tell me the truth. I appreciate your instincts about people and your detective skills. But if I can't trust you to tell me the truth, I can't have you tagging along on my interviews."

"I've been truthful with you. Except for this morning. You want the truth? I didn't want to upset you that Heath saw my house before you. But, in all fairness, I have known Heath a lot longer and feel like he's family. It is no different for him to see my house and all my flaws than my mother."

His eyes narrowed. "What do you mean about

flaws?"

She closed her eyes, drew in a deep breath, and let it out. "I'm damaged goods and I didn't want you to see all the handicapped bars in my house." She waved. "Drive up to the house before they wonder what's going on."

He stared at her for a couple beats more and then drove on up to the house. "We'll continue this discussion after we talk to Mrs. Silva."

"Goodie," she said under her breath as she slipped out of the vehicle.

♠ ♣ ♥ ♦

Stacy Silva sat in the living room surrounded by family members. It appeared all of the Rose family had converged on Melba and Butch to help Stacy grieve.

Quinn and Dela stood inside the door, scanning the twenty people. Quinn stepped forward. "We'd like to have a few words with Mrs. Silva."

Ben crossed the room, standing in front of Quinn. "She's not up to speaking to you."

"How about you let Mrs. Silva make that decision," Quinn said, his anger from their conversation still showing in his gray eyes.

Dela slipped around the two cocks, figuratively, bumping chests, and stopped beside Stacy. "I have a couple of questions I'd like to ask you. Is there someplace we can go that's private?"

The woman nodded, stood, and led Dela through the kitchen and out the back door. The wind was cold this high up from the valley floor. Dela wished she'd worn a coat.

"Follow me. We'll get out of the wind." Stacy trotted toward a small wooden structure at the edge of the forest.

Dela followed as best she could over the rough ground littered with small pine tree limbs and pinecones which hindered her balance. At the building, she ducked through the door and found two child-sized chairs and a table.

"This is the playhouse my cousins and I used to play in." Stacy's gaze roamed around the inside of the structure. "We pretended to be teachers and marry handsome men who took us away from the reservation." Her gaze landed on Dela. "I was the only one who made my dream come true." A tear glistened in the corner of her eye. "And yet, I keep coming back to the rez and now I no longer have a handsome husband."

Dela let the woman reflect on her grief for a couple of minutes before asking, "I know we asked you yesterday, when you were in shock, about any enemies your husband might have. Now that you've had time to gather yourself, have you come up with any names?"

Stacy started to shake her head and stopped. "If you had asked me this before they started all these summits about the dam breaching, I would have said, no. But since the summits, Kevin has received threats, we've had dead fish left on our porch and put in our cars if we forgot to lock them."

"Did he keep the threats?" Dela asked.

"He turned them into his boss at the power company. Steve Wallen. You could ask him for copies, I'd think." Stacy hugged her arms around her. "Kevin took the job at the power company to help them see the harm that came to the wildlife and nature. Slowly, he'd come home saying, yes, some wildlife was harmed but the greater good came to the humans. It saddened me that he was letting the corporations change his mind." She sniffed. "Then when he brought up that breaching was the best way to save the fish, I thought he was back to thinking for the good of The People. But the other night when his only answer to me when I confronted him, was 'What do you think?,' I felt betrayed."

Dela nodded. "I can understand. You think you know a person and they do something that seems out of character. Who told you he'd changed his mind about the breaching?"

"Tommy Darkhorse. He said he'd heard Kevin talking with one of the power company people, saying 'yes, he knew the right thing to do.'" She peered at Dela. "That sounds like he was siding with the power company. When I questioned him, that's when we had the fight at the blackjack table."

"You only heard this from Tommy Darkhorse? What made you think he was telling the truth?" Dela had thought she'd say Connie Oswood. That it was Darkhorse she had heard it from, after the man said he'd talked it over with the victim, had her baffled.

The woman blushed. "Tommy has been keeping me up to date on the outcome of the summits."

"Why is that? I would think your husband's word would have been the truth." Dela studied the woman. What wasn't she telling?

"After the first summit, which I didn't attend, I found lipstick on Kevin's collar and a note tucked into his jacket pocket. It said, 'You know what to do.'"

"You thought he was having an affair and going to leave you?" Dela questioned.

She nodded, tears in her eyes. "When I asked him

about it, he said the note was from someone threatening him to go against the breaching and he said he had no idea how the lipstick got on his collar. I told him I believed him, then I contacted Tommy. He and one of my brothers are friends. He planned to attend all the summits, and said he'd be pleased to keep an eye on Kevin."

"What did he report back?" Dela asked.

"That there was a woman at all the summits who pushed herself on all the men who were for breaching. That she tried to sway their judgment. He said, she'd even tried to get him to let her into his bed. That he'd witnessed her coming on to Kevin and my husband walked away." She sniffed. "I believed him when he told me he was true to me and I believe it now."

Dela nodded. It fit with what they'd seen on the footage of the victim and Connie at this conference. Now to bring up the complicated question. "How well do you know your cousin, Ben?"

"Ben?" Stacy stared at her for several seconds. "We met as children. Have seen one another at family gatherings over the years. Why?"

"He seems a bit overprotective of you." She didn't want to say what she really thought. That he seemed infatuated with her.

Stacy laughed. "He's always been a bit intense. I just laugh it off."

Intense. Dela thought that was an odd way to describe her cousin. "How does he feel about the dam breaching?"

"He's for it. He says the dams should never have been put in. Not everyone on reservations have power so why should the Whiteman worry about not having enough." She shrugged. "He throws himself into the causes. And has made a difference for many."

Pride dripped off her words. She thought he was a man who helped make changes. Could he have decided that his cousin's husband was interfering in his cause?

"Dela?" Quinn called.

She stood. "My ride summons me. Thank you for talking with me. We're doing our best to find out who killed your husband."

"I appreciate that. It will help the healing process to know who and why. Right now, my mind just spins with why." The woman's face slackened and her eyes grew moist.

"Hang in there. I'll keep you updated."

"Dela!" Quinn called again with less patience.

"I'm here." She ducked out of the playhouse and walked across the yard to the special agent.

"What were you doing?" His gaze remained on the playhouse.

"Stacy and I were having a quiet conversation without her possessive cousin around. How did your conversation with him go?"

Quinn headed to the side of the house. "He said he didn't know who killed Kevin. He hadn't talked to the victim for several years."

Dela followed him back to the vehicle. Once they were seated, she repeated what she'd learned.

"It appears Darkhorse didn't tell us everything." Was all Quinn had to say about her conversation with Stacy.

"Did you not hear me say that our victim had been threatened and had turned the emails over to his boss? I'm surprised we haven't heard from him yet." She'd thought it odd that no one had mentioned Kevin's boss offering to help. Especially if there had been threats against his employee.

"I heard you. I have an agent in the Boise area talking with him today."

"Steve Wallen?" she asked, to make sure it was the correct person.

"I don't know thc name."

"Well, make sure that's who the agent talks to." Dela leaned back in the seat. Her phone buzzed. "Hello?"

"It's Kenny, I'm heading home thought I'd give you a rundown."

"Go ahead." She closed her eyes and listened to Kenny tell her things ran smooth other than an older couple who came by bus were left behind and had to be put up for the night and the bus company called to retrieve them this morning. They were now gone. Everything else ran as usual. And Detective Jones was roaming around talking to the Save Our Fish attendees.

"Thank you. I'll get back as soon as I can." She ended the call. "Any chance you can get back to the casino faster than we traveled to the Rose residence."

"Something wrong at the casino?" Quinn accelerated the vehicle.

"Only Detective Dick nosing around." She really didn't like the man. He would do all he could to put a bad light on the casino. Why he had it out for her and the casino, she'd probably never find out, but she needed this job and didn't want him spouting off about the homicide to chase customers away.

With Quinn driving fast and intent on the road, she was thinking about the next phase of remodeling Travis had planned when Quinn cleared his throat.

She swung her face around to stare at him.

"What did you mean by handicapped bars all over your house?" His gaze did a quick scan of her before returning to the road.

"I didn't want you to know that I lost my lower right leg. That's why I wasn't able to finish out my twenty years. Damn IED ripped through the Jeep injuring every one of us who were in it." She swallowed. Her injuries were minor compared to some of her friends.

"I'm sorry." He glanced over, then back to the road. "Maybe you should have stayed with your mom a while longer."

"Shit no!" Anger replaced her embarrassment. "She was always there as if she expected me to fall over every time I took a step. I couldn't stay there and gain strength and confidence. Getting this house…it's making me feel normal. Or as normal as I'll ever get."

"She just loves you and doesn't want you to get hurt," he said.

"I know. But I can't go through life missing out because my mom thinks I might get hurt."

Quinn turned into the casino parking lot, pulled into a parking slot, and faced her. "Why didn't you want me to know about your disability?"

"Because I don't want you treating me differently. I don't want you compensating for my lack of mobility or not allowing me to do what needs to be done for fear 'I'll hurt myself.'" She sighed. "I want you to treat me like you did in Iraq. I'm no different, I just don't move as fast."

He peered into her eyes. "You want me to boss you

around and override your decisions?"

"Hell no! We've been working together here just fine so far. I don't want you to change that." She scowled. "We need to get in and see what damage Detective Dick has done."

She exited the vehicle and marched to the casino entrance. Quinn caught up to her as the interior doors swooshed open. It was a busy Friday afternoon. She had business to take care of as head of security, but she also had a murder to solve that could influence if she continued to be head of security.

Dela turned her mic on and slipped her earbud into her ear. "Who has eyes on Detective Dick?" she asked.

"He's in the events center talking to the attendees," Ross replied.

"Thanks," she said into the mic. "Come on," she said to Quinn, heading toward the events center. "He's in here. Do you think he's had time to read through your report?"

"It would have taken longer for him to read through mine than it took me to read through his. He just had names and 'not a witness' by the name." Quinn strode by her to open the door into the largest conference room.

"That sounds like how he does all of his work," she muttered and stepped into the room. The detective had taken over the table she and Quinn had used the day before.

They walked down between the aisles of chairs.

Jerry Timmons, one of the speakers, jumped up from his seat and hurried up the aisle toward them. "I thought you said we could continue the summit? This detective has been taking up all of our time questioning people one by one. We might as well all go home and regroup for the next one."

Dela glared at Detective Dick, who sat in his chair grinning at them.

"I'm sorry, for this inconvenience. But we are trying to find out who killed your main speaker," Quinn said, calming down the man.

Dela continued down to Dick. "I thought we talked to all of these people yesterday, did you learn something new this morning?"

The detective narrowed his eyes. "Yesterday, you and the FBI talked to the people I'm talking to today. I thought Quinn's report was slim on all the information you'd gathered."

Dela snorted and said, "I doubt it could be much slimmer than yours. A name and 'not a witness' written next to it."

The man sitting at the table grinned.

"You can go," Dick said, waving the man away. "What were you and the agent doing this morning?"

"We had another talk with the victim's wife. We figured she'd had a night to calm down and could give us some better information." Dela took a seat next to the detective and pulled his notes, which were Quinn's report, toward her.

"Did you learn anything new?" Dick asked as Quinn joined them.

"The victim had been receiving threats. His wife said he gave them to his boss."

Dela settled her gaze on Quinn. "Now would be a good time to see what Shaffer dug up." She stood.

Quinn tapped his report. "This should have told you all you need to know about the attendees other than running background checks. Why don't you let them get back to their summit?"

"I have a homicide investigation to conduct," Detective Dick said, glaring at Quinn.

"You'll learn more by digging around and seeing if any of the attendees have records or a history of taking their causes to an extreme." Quinn pulled a pen out of his pocket and wrote a name on the top of the report. "And while you're at it, run a check on Ben Gibbons. He has a temper and from the way he talked, he's been following these summits."

Dick's jaw dropped open. "Butch and Melba Rose's grandson?"

"Yes. Him." Quinn motioned for Dela to walk away. When they were headed back up the aisle he said, "Let's go to my office. That's where Shaffer is working on the computer."

"Can't you just call him and get the information?" She didn't want to leave, she needed to get her usual work done.

"He said it would be easier to show us." Quinn stopped. "Why don't you want to leave?"

"I have some responsibilities I need to take care of here. Can you have Shaffer bring the laptop here? That would give me some time to get things done and still sit in on what he's found."

"I'll call and see if that will work. Where will you be?" He drew his phone out of his inside breast pocket.

Dela pointed to the security offices. "In there working on next week's schedule and checking in with the leads in the various areas." She didn't wait for his reply, she headed to her office. As much as she'd rather keep gathering information about the homicide, she had to put the casino first.

Chapter Nine

An hour later, Quinn walked into the security offices with Special Agent Shaffer behind him. "Where can Milo set this up?"

Dela glanced at the large laptop under the agent's arm. "In the interview room." She nodded to a door to the left of where she sat finishing up the scheduling. She'd talked to all her leads before working on the schedule. It was something she could have worked on at home, but she preferred to not have any casino business on her home computer. The security here was much more sophisticated than what she had at home.

The two men entered the room. She figured she had another five or ten minutes to finish up before Shaffer had the computer set up and ready to show her anything.

Rosie walked through the door.

"Are you leaving already?" Dela asked, before noticing the basket with a sandwich and chips in one hand and a drink in the other.

"No. That sexy FBI man ordered this to be delivered to you." The playful woman winked. "I think you better keep tabs on him before someone, like me, steals him away."

Dela laughed. "I told you yesterday, you are more than welcome to him." Even as she said the words, and as much as she cared for the woman, a little ember of jealousy burned in her gut.

"I don't have to be told twice," Rosie said, handing her the food and drink. "The next time he comes by, I'll invite him to my cousin Sharon's birthday party."

"He should enjoy that," Dela said. "Thanks." She closed her monitor and walked over to the small room just as the door opened.

"Thanks, Rosie," Quinn said and smiled.

"You're welcome. Come by and see me later." Rosie giggled and danced toward the door.

"What was that all about?" Quinn asked, moving into the interview room so she could step through the door.

"She's planning to ask you to her cousin's birthday party." She smiled and sat at the table on the right side of Special Agent Shaffer.

"It looks like we're working together again," Shaffer said.

"Yes. Too bad it couldn't be you and me and leave Quinn back at the office," she said, before biting into her ham sandwich.

"I'll figure that is your empty stomach talking," Quinn said, sitting in the chair on the other side of Shaffer.

Dela didn't say anything, just continued to eat and

sip her soda as Shaffer explained what he'd found on the computer.

"From the charts, reports from other environmentalists and wildlife experts, and the letter the victim had typed up, he was for the breaching of the dams. He also had an extensive file he'd collected on how the power company could continue to profit and make electricity with the dams taken away. I'd say the victim was working hard to make things right for both sides of this issue."

Dela thought about that. "Did he send the letter to his boss?"

"I couldn't find anywhere in his email that he'd sent it or any of the information he'd gathered." Shaffer tapped the keyboard.

"It sounds like he was keeping his research secret. Why?" Dela glanced at Quinn and then Shaffer. They both appeared lost in their thoughts. "Do you think his agreeing with both sides got him killed? I mean, the breaching group would be angry with him, if, as several said, he was seen agreeing with the power company people. And the power company people could have seen him talking to, say, Darkhorse, and he's smiling, nodding, and shaking the victim's hand. It would have made both sides upset to see the main speaker and the man whose word would determine the outcome of the fish and dams looking as if he was just agreeing with everything."

Quinn stared at her. "It opens up the suspect pool even more. If this was his behavior at all of the summits, he could have hundreds of people who don't like him."

"Or someone saw his letter to the power company

and didn't like his recommendation," Shaffer added. "The time stamp on the last time the document was opened was one a.m. the morning he was killed."

"There is that." Dela shoved to her feet. "We haven't checked the video surveillance on the tenth-floor hall. It would tell us who came and went from that room."

Quinn stood. "Milo, did you find any threats on the computer?"

"There were some in the email trash. It looked like he'd forwarded them to someone at the power company."

"Make copies of those and contact the person he sent them to. We need to see how many threats there were and if any of them came from the same person." Quinn motioned for Dela to exit the room ahead of him.

In the security offices, he led the way to the door out onto the casino floor. "Why didn't we check the hallway footage before? It would tell us exactly who was the last person to enter and exit that room."

Dela stepped out on the casino floor, listening for anything that sounded off. The clang and ding of the slot machines rang out over the background Native American flute music. People were arriving to spend the weekend at the casino. The drone of voices added to the chaos. "Because we were busy chasing down the people who had arguments with the victim."

She continued along the wall to the obscure box where she tapped her security clearance and the wall opened, allowing them entrance. The door swished closed behind them. The hum of monitors and faint shuffling as the surveillance team sat up straight, was a welcome change from the noise of the casino floor.

"How goes the hunt?" Lionel asked.

"Slow but sure," Dela replied. "Is Marty in his office?"

"Yeah."

"Thanks." She continued through the room full of monitors and knocked on the head of surveillance's door.

"Yo!" Marty called out.

Dela entered with Quinn on her heels.

"What do you need me to look up?" Marty was tipped back in his chair, a clipboard in his hands.

"We need to see who came and went from room ten-twenty the night of the murder." Dela pulled out her usual chair and propped her leg on the box under the table.

"I figured you'd come looking for that eventually." Marty slid the clipboard in a slot on a shelf below the three monitors and began bringing the middle monitor to life. "What time do you want to start at?"

She glanced at Quinn. "Ten?"

"When did the husband and wife get in an argument?" he asked.

"Before eleven." She hadn't glanced at her watch to check the time since it wasn't an incident that needed to be reported.

"Then ten's a good time to start." Quinn had settled into the chair on the other side of Marty.

"Ten it is."

The hallway on the tenth floor appeared on the monitor.

"The room you're looking for is down the hall. I'm not sure exactly which one it is since we can't see the numbers from this angle." Marty apologized.

"When Stacy enters the room, we'll know which one to watch." Dela tried counting the doors. She was pretty sure the one they wanted to watch was about halfway down the hall.

"Go ahead and fast forward until we see her," Quinn said.

Harvey Beecher walked down the hall and entered a room. "Stop." Dela counted the doors from the corner. It was the third one on the left. She grabbed a piece of paper and quickly sketched the hallway. "Okay, continue."

Before Stacy showed up, another person of interest walked down the hall and entered the door next to Beecher's room. It was Connie Oswood.

"Do you think all the people attending the summit are on the tenth floor?" Quinn asked as if talking to himself.

Stacy hurried down the hall and entered the room just beyond Beecher on the same side. Five minutes later the victim arrived, letting himself into the room.

"Fast forward until one of them comes out or someone else walks down the hall." Quinn leaned forward, his forearms on the table as if it would help him see better.

Tommy Darkhorse walked down the hall, stopped outside of the Silvas room, listened, and then entered the room across the hall.

Quinn leaned back. "Darkhorse never said anything about listening at the door."

"He also said he didn't know the room where the victim was staying." Dela narrowed her eyes wondering what else the man hadn't said.

Twenty minutes later, the victim left the room and

strode down the hallway. Connie Oswood's door opened and she hurried down the hall.

"She was spying on the Silvas and is heading after Kevin," Dela said. The woman's actions reassured Dela she hadn't lost her ability to read people. The woman was up to something.

They watched the video. Stacy left the room about 12:30 with a small bag. Darkhorse stepped out of his room when she was out of sight of the camera and walked across the hall to knock on the Silvas door. When he didn't get a response, he wandered down the hall.

"Fast forward to when the victim returns to the room." Quinn's tone sounded like he was thinking about something.

Around 2 a.m. the victim strolled down the hall with Connie's arm hooked through his. He stopped at her door. She unlocked her door and unhooked their arms before she walked into her room. Silva slowly walked over to his door. There wasn't any hint of attraction for the woman that Dela could tell. He had just been a gentleman and escorted the woman to her room.

Darkhorse appeared and walked up to the door the victim had just shut. He knocked and waited about a minute. Silva opened the door and waved the man in. The meeting looked natural and unemotional. Twenty minutes later Darkhorse exited and the door closed behind him.

"He didn't pull the door closed. It was closed by someone on the inside," Dela offered.

"I saw that. Which means when he left, Silva was alive."

Dela noted the time stamp on the video. 2:36 a.m.

Marty fast-forwarded. No one else entered the room until the maid found the body.

"We need to speak with Tommy Darkhorse." Quinn stood, and Dela thanked Marty for his help.

"We saw the door close from the inside. Tommy didn't kill Silva," Dela said, as they walked through the room full of monitors.

"No, but he might shine more light on what they talked about and if there might have been someone else in the room."

"How? We watched the hallway from ten on. We saw who came and went." Dela followed him over to the registration desk.

"There had to be someone else in the room." Quinn stopped at the desk and smiled at Faith. "Can you see if Tommy Darkhorse left a cell phone number on his registration?"

"Sure thing." Faith smiled at Quinn and gave Dela a sly wink. Her friend tapped on the keyboard and then wrote on a sticky note. "Here is the phone number he left for a message about when his room would be available."

"Thank you," Quinn said, taking the slip of paper and walking over to a quiet corner.

"You're not going to go huddle in the corner with him?" Faith asked.

Dela rolled her eyes. "I wish everyone would stop trying to fix me up with him."

Faith's eyes widened.

Before Dela could turn around, a familiar voice said, "Fix you up with who?"

She slowly pivoted and stared into Heath's eyes.

"My friends are all trying to fix me up with any male who comes within ten feet of me. So be careful."

Heath chuckled. "They are all just worried about you living alone."

"Yeah, right. What brought you back here?" Dela glanced at the file in his hand.

"Some of the backgrounds on people attending the summit came back and some interesting reports from the lab on the evidence picked up in the room." Heath nodded to where Quinn was frowning as he talked on the phone. "I'm pretty sure he wants in on this."

Dela sighed. "I suppose so."

Heath laughed.

Quinn's head spun on his neck as his gaze landed on the two of them.

"Looks like he knows you're here now." She wondered at how having Heath back in her life had brought a new joy. They had always been able to joke around and have a good time. She'd missed that ever since she'd pushed him away.

The special agent shoved his phone in his pocket and strode over to where she and Heath still stood by the registration desk. Faith should have had a bag of popcorn, she was watching them with such avid interest.

"What have you found?" Quinn asked, stopping three feet in front of Heath. It was like two bull elk having a standoff during rutting season.

The image made Dela bite back the chuckle that bubbled in her throat.

"I have some interesting background checks and evidence picked up at the crime scene." Heath held up the file.

"Let's get a booth in the coffee shop." Quinn started to walk away.

"Why not the security office?" Dela asked.

"I need some coffee." Quinn continued walking.

She shrugged and fell in step alongside Heath. "Has Detective Dick given you the case?"

"Not really. Chief Steele asked me to help with the investigation, and Detective Jones said he had somewhere to be and walked out of the station."

"It sounds like the chief has figured out Jones doesn't really want to do his job." This news made Dela happy. Maybe now more people on the rez would get the help they needed knowing they didn't have to deal with Detective Dick.

"I was brought onto the force to be his replacement." Heath smiled.

"Nice! Congratulations!" Dela was happy to know her friend would be sticking around and would have a chance for advancement.

"Don't get too excited. I have a feeling this assignment is to assess how well I work with the Feds and how good of an investigator I am. The chief did say, he'd be happy to see me crack this before you or him." They had stepped into the coffee shop to find Quinn already seated and glaring at their entrance.

"You know where my loyalties lie." She winked and walked over to the booth where a waitress was pouring three cups of coffee. Dela waited for Heath to slide in before she sat on the edge of the seat.

"What did you find?" Quinn asked, lifting his cup of coffee up as his gaze moved from her to Heath.

"Harvey Beecher has had two assault charges filed on him in the last five years. One was recently when a power company representative wanted to survey his land to see what kind of damage the dam breaching would do." Heath pushed that report across the table to Quinn.

"Tommy Darkhorse has been arrested for unlawful protests six times in the last ten years. He was one of the protesters arrested at the access pipeline in South Dakota." He pushed several pages over to the special agent.

"Connie Oswood hasn't been arrested, but she has been hauled in twice on conspiracy charges. However, there was never enough evidence to take her to court." Heath shuffled those pages to Dela.

She glanced over them, noting the conspiracy had been with the power company paying for her room. That could mean she was sent here to make sure the breaching wouldn't happen.

"What about the evidence the lab found?" Quinn asked, glancing up from the reports on the two men.

"Sage ash was also found on the floor around the chair where the body was found. The lack of matches or lighter in the room and the smudging leans towards this having been premeditated rather than a spur-of-the-moment rage. They also vacuumed up hair. The ones with follicle matter are being run for DNA. And they found an earring back, which could be from his wife or a past guest in the room." Heath glanced at Dela. "We know the vacuum cleaners in these places don't have the suction of the ones the crime scene investigators use."

She nodded. "Any prints on the lamp or cord?"

"None on the lamp and only partials on the cord." Heath peered at Quinn. "Any idea how long it takes the state lab in Clackamas to get the clothing processed?"

"If there's a backlog, could be a few days." Quinn stared at the paper in front of him. "Did you do a background check on Jerry Timmons?"

"Yes. It came back clean. Why?"

Quinn held up a paper with a photo of a group being arrested in South Dakota. He pointed to a person just behind Tommy. "That looks like Timmons. The way his shoulders look...he's in cuffs too."

Chapter Ten

"We need to chat with Darkhorse and Timmons," Quinn said.

Dela waved the papers she had on Connie Oswood. "What about her?"

"We saw her walk into her room and not come out again on the surveillance tapes." Quinn finished off his coffee and stood.

"She could have had something to do with it. She may not have strangled him, but I bet you she worked the person up who did do it." Dela stood. "Ms. Oswood needs to be interviewed again. Especially, now that we know more about her."

Quinn stared at her. "We can talk to her after the other two."

"Fine. Did you find out if Tommy Darkhorse is in the casino when you called him?" She moved out of the way to let Heath exit the booth.

"We're to meet him in ten minutes at the event

center. His talk will be over then." Quinn tossed money on the table and walked toward the front of the café.

"Is he always this grumpy?" Heath whispered as they followed.

"He's prickly most of the time. If this didn't involve the casino, I'd back out and let you have all the fun of hanging out with him." Dela followed Quinn across the casino floor, wondering what was up his ass. Usually, they got along just fine. She caught a glimpse of Heath in her peripheral vision and realized Quinn didn't like sharing her with the tribal policeman. Detective Dick always kept his distance from them, doing nothing. Heath was determined to prove to his chief that he was the man to take over Dick's position. Quinn would just have to get over it.

They entered the event center. Tommy Darkhorse stepped out of the main conference room speaking with an attendee.

Quinn stopped about fifteen feet from the two. She and Heath stood beside him, waiting.

Tommy glanced their way, ended his conversation with the person, and walked toward them. "What is this about Special Agent?"

"We have some questions for you. Is anyone in there?" Quinn tipped his head in the direction of the smaller conference room.

"I don't believe so. Is that where you want to ask me questions?"

"If you don't mind. We've uncovered some information that we'd like to hear your side about." Quinn motioned for Tommy to lead the way.

When they were all seated around a table, Quinn held his hand out for the folder Heath held.

Her friend, and tribal officer, handed it to him without batting an eye. Dela wondered if he was being compliant because Quinn was FBI or because he was new and getting a feel for the dynamics he would be working with in years to come.

"We watched a video of the hallway outside Kevin Silva's room. It appears you tried to talk with him twice, and the third time, when he came back to his room after two in the morning, you were let in and stayed for about twenty minutes. What were you so anxious to talk to the victim about?" Quinn had pulled out his notepad.

Dela's lips turned up, noting Heath had his logbook out as well.

"I wanted to make sure what Connie was going around saying wasn't true. And to let Kevin know she was doing everything she could to make his wife think the two of them were having an affair." Tommy slammed a fist down on the table. "That woman is up to no good."

"The last time we talked, you didn't call her by her name. You said the blonde woman as if you didn't know her." Dela stared into the man's eyes. "Is that because you didn't want us to know you were watching her and Kevin for Mrs. Silva?"

Tommy shook his head. "I didn't want you to think Stacy could have killed her husband. She loves him. She'd never harm him."

Dela gave one slight nod. "You were the last one to see Kevin alive. No one else went in or out of his room after you did."

Tommy's eyes narrowed. "Hey, hey. I didn't kill him. He was alive when I left that room. He said he had to tweak the end of the talk he was giving the next day and then he was going to try to sleep. I told him he looked like he needed to sleep and then tweak his speech." The man shook his head slowly. "He told me his wife didn't believe him when he told her he was for the breaching. He planned to tell everyone the next day what his findings were."

"Was this the last summit?" Heath asked.

"No. There is one more planned. But I think Kevin had found all he needed to prove breaching is the right thing to do." Tommy leveled his gaze on all three of them. "I know he was worried about what his boss would say. Kevin said he needed to call him before he made the announcement."

"Was there anyone else in the room when you were visiting with the victim?" Quinn asked.

Tommy stared at him as if Quinn had asked him a stupid question. "There was only me and Kevin in that room."

"What about the bathroom? Was the door open or closed?" Quinn continued.

"You think someone else was in there when we were talking? I was there quite a while. I didn't hear or see anyone, other than Kevin." The man stared at the table. "Do you think the killer was hiding in the bathroom? Does that mean he could be after me, thinking I saw or heard something?"

"Like you said, twenty minutes is a long time for someone to not make a noise that you would have heard," Dela said, to put the man's mind at rest since Quinn, nor Heath, seemed to think it was necessary.

"You do have a history of getting arrested and assaulting people at protests." Quinn said.

"This isn't a protest. This is two sides calmly talking out our differences." Tommy glared at Quinn.

"How can you talk calmly to the powerful power companies that have the money to pay government officials to let things continue as they have been?" Heath asked.

Tommy studied Heath. "You are working for the government. I work for the government, but I'm damn sure neither one of us would take money to hurt the environment. There are many Indigenous people involved in this effort. I can't see the government getting away with taking bribes on this. Not with all the other stuff that has been going on."

Dela had a feeling he was talking about the Indigenous children's skeletons being found at Indian schools across Canada and bringing up the question of whether the U.S. had the same at its centuries old Indian schools.

Heath nodded. "Our voices are finally being heard. The government can try to hide things, but we will dig it all up." He stared at Quinn.

"You didn't come here to put pressure on Mr. Silva?" Quinn asked.

"No. I was welcomed here to speak for the native fish." Tommy glared at Quinn.

"Did you see or hear anything that gave you the impression someone might do something radical to stop the summit or the breaching?" Dela asked. At least a third of the attendees seemed to have been going to all the conferences. She figured word would have gotten around if someone was making accusations.

"Beecher has been at the last two. He has been loud about how the fish aren't worth ruining people's farms.

He threatened Kevin at the summit in Lewiston three weeks ago. I thought he'd been banned from further participation." Tommy peered at all three of them. "He has a temper."

"He didn't go near the victim's room that night. Just in his room on the same hall." As she said it, a light clicked in Dela's brain. "That room had a connecting door." She retraced her movements when she was at the crime scene. "But the connecting door was on the opposite side of Harvey Beecher's room." Dela pulled out her cell phone, walking away from the three men. She called Faith at the registration desk.

"Hey, why are you calling me? You just walked away from here with two hot men." Her friend giggled.

"Can you tell me who is staying in the room that connects with ten-twenty?" Dela didn't have time for girl talk.

Tapping of keys told her Faith was looking.

"Jerry Timmons was in that room. He checked out early this morning."

"Thank you." She ended the call and stalked back to the table. All three men stared at her. She was pretty sure her anger at not thinking about this sooner had her face red and contorted.

Quinn dismissed Darkhorse, who quickly rose and walked away. "What did you learn?" Quinn asked.

"Jerry Timmons was in the room connected to the crime scene and he left this morning." She slapped her hand on her thigh. "I should have picked up on the connecting room sooner."

"I checked it out," Heath said. "It was locked from Silva's side, and when I unlocked it and checked the other door, it was locked as well. I didn't think anyone had come in that way and, like you, figured it had to be the wife."

Dela shook her head. "I don't think she did it. She loved him and is having trouble coming to grips with his death. But I missed the connecting door until now, I could be wrong about her as well."

"Stop berating yourself. I'm going to find Timmons's home address and we'll go have a talk with him," Quinn said, pulling out his phone and texting.

"While you do that, Heath and I can go talk to Connie Oswood." She motioned for Heath to follow her.

"They'll text me his information. I'll go, too." Quinn shoved his phone in his pocket and led the way out of the room.

It was evident the special agent didn't want to miss a moment visiting with the sexy Ms. Oswood. Dela kept that thought to herself as she called Marty to get a location on the woman.

"Surprise, surprise, she's in the Pony hitting up on someone," Dela relayed to Quinn and Heath.

Quinn stopped outside the grill. "You're not going to be bitchy the whole time we talk to her, are you?"

Dela crossed her arms. "You aren't going to drool on your tie while you talk to her, are you?"

Heath burst out laughing. When he caught his breath, he said, "Would you two sleep together and get whatever this is out of your system?" He passed them and walked into the bar.

Dela glared at Heath's back, following him. She didn't want to see what Quinn thought of her friend's comment.

Connie Oswood smiled as Heath approached her.

The man, sitting at the table with her, frowned.

"Ms. Oswood, we," Heath motioned to Dela and Quinn, "have some questions for you."

The woman's gaze flit right by Dela and landed on Quinn. "Come have a seat. Randal was just leaving."

The man's round face didn't say he was about to leave. His eyes narrowed, and he ran a thick hand through his gray hair.

When the man didn't budge, Connie shrugged. "Or he can stay. I don't have anything to say that can't be heard by one and all."

Quinn took a seat to Connie's left. Heath motioned for Dela to take the seat to the woman's right. Heath remained standing between Dela and Randal.

"We noticed Mr. Silva walked you to your room the night he died," Quinn started.

Randal gasped. "You knew the man who died here?"

Connie patted the man's hand resting on the table. "I didn't kill him."

"Did he say anything about what he planned to do the rest of the night?" Quinn finished.

"Well, he did tell me that he would never take me up on my offer because he loved his wife." She winked at Randal and Quinn.

"Did he mention anything about needing to make calls or talk to anyone?" Dela asked. She was sure the woman wasn't telling them everything.

"He said he had to call his boss and finish writing up his talk for the next day. You know, with as many summits as he'd attended, you would have thought he'd just give the same talk." Connie picked up her drink and sipped.

"Would him calling his boss give you any cause to worry?" Dela asked.

The woman narrowed her eyes. "What do you mean?"

"We know your room here is being paid for by the largest power company in Idaho. If Mr. Silva was going to call his boss, I would think you would have wanted to know what he was going to say." Dela watched the woman's eyelids slowly lower, hiding her emotions. "After all, you're here to make sure the power company gets what they want."

"What do you mean by that? I'm here to report on the outcome of these summits for the paper. That's all." Connie speared her with glaring eyes.

"No, that's what you tell everyone. If a power company is paying for your room, your loyalty lies with them. Did you report to someone that night what Mr. Silva was leaning toward? The breaching?" Dela saw the flicker of surprise before she lowered her lashes again.

"He never told me what he'd decided. I thought I still had a chance to make him see the power companies would treat him well if he favored not breaching the dams." She raised her lashes. "His wife has expensive tastes. I'm sure he would have realized he'd be out of a job if he went against what his company wanted."

Dela shot a glance at Quinn. They didn't know if the victim had sent his recommendation to his boss.

Quinn must have had the same idea. "Thank you for your time." He stood.

Dela slid off the tall chair and landed harder than she liked on her prosthesis. A hand on her elbow steadied her. She pulled her elbow out of Heath's grasp and walked out of the Pony Bar and Grill.

Chapter Eleven

Dela followed Quinn over to the security office. It was evident he planned to see what Shaffer had come up with in regards to the boss getting the report from the victim.

They entered the office.

"Dela isn't here right now," Tammie, one of the security guards said.

"She's behind me," Quinn said, heading into the small room to the side.

Stopping beside the woman, Dela pointed to Heath. "This is Tribal Officer Heath Seaver. He's working on the homicide with the FBI and myself. He may come in here looking for me, don't throw him out."

Heath held out a hand.

Tammie shook hands with him. "It's good to see the tribal police have manners, unlike other law enforcement officers around here." She gave a pointed scowl at the door Quinn had entered.

Heath smiled. "I'm just like everyone else."

Tammie laughed. "I like him."

Dela nodded and they hurried into the room to see what Quinn was finding out.

"According to Mr. Wallen, he hasn't received any emails from the victim. He did send over a file with the threats the victim had sent to him." Shaffer held up about a dozen papers. "I had them printed out so you could all see them without crowding around the computer."

"Thanks," Dela said, as Quinn handed her a couple of pages, as well as Heath.

They all read in silence for a few minutes.

"Do any of them sound like the same person sent them?" Quinn asked.

Shaffer shook his head. "They all seem to come from different people. I tried running a program on them for similarities and none came up."

"And you're sure this Wallen never received the report for the breaching?" Heath asked.

Shaffer studied Heath. "That's what I said."

"Dela, I'm on duty," she heard in her earbud. Dela handed the pages to Quinn. "I have to go meet with Kenny. If you come up with anything interesting, give me a call."

While she wanted to get this murder solved, she also had a job that needed to be done. She stepped into the security office and smiled at her second in command, Kenny Proudhorse.

"I didn't mean for you to stop looking for the killer," he said.

"We're kind of stuck at the moment. I'd rather deal with casino business." They spent the next hour going over extra security for the following month when they had a political function happening at the casino. As Kenny stood to go out and canvas the casino floor, the door to the small room opened.

None of the men who walked out looked particularly happy. She wondered what they had decided in her absence.

Quinn walked over to her. "Timmons lives in Cambridge, Idaho. Works out of Boise. I'm headed over there to talk to him tomorrow. I'll pick you up at eight."

She held up a hand. "I've got a job to do here."

Quinn scanned her face. "When have you backed down on going after the evidence in a homicide?"

"I'm not backing down. You didn't ask me if I wanted to go. You told me I was going. I'm not on the FBI payroll." She glanced at Heath. "Or the Tribal Police payroll."

"I wasn't going to say anything, but Bernie called me," Kenny said.

Dela whipped around and stared at her second in command. "What did he call you about?"

"He wanted to know if you were keeping this latest death out of the paper and working on finding out that the casino had nothing to do with the murder." The large Umatilla man shrugged.

Dela let out a long sigh. "I guess I'm going with you tomorrow. If Bernie thinks I need to be on top of this, then I better do my due diligence." When she turned, Heath was watching her.

"I have work to do until then." She cleared all non-security people out of the office and then sat down at her desk. Driving for three hours with Quinn might give her time to figure out why he didn't like Heath.

After tackling the rest of the paperwork for her job, she stretched and walked out to the casino floor. The Friday night crowd was in full swing. Dela made the rounds, asking her crew how things were going. She smiled at Albert at the valet station and ordered a sandwich to go from the deli.

"You and Heath going to get back together?" Rosie asked, handing Dela her sandwich.

"Why do you ask?" Dela didn't like all the interest around her past boyfriend and herself.

"Just wondering. He is more pleasant than that hunky fed. And you do have a past." The woman studied her. "I can tell you still have feelings for him. But you're also fighting your feelings for Mr. Hunky."

Dela shook her head. "I don't have time to think about feelings. Bernie wants this latest murder solved." She walked away, wondering how she'd thought coming back to live on the rez would be easier than the outside world. Everyone here butted into your business.

♠ ♣ ♥ ♦

Dela ate her sandwich on the drive home and immediately changed into her running prosthesis and jogging pants. With Mugshot on a leash, they set off on their usual jogging path around the community of Tutuilla Flats. This evening ritual, that she didn't get to do every evening, was one of the reasons she'd moved here. She took a left out of her property and jogged down to the next intersection, taking in the view of the Blue Mountains and Cabbage Hill. Making another left and following the road, she jogged by a small farm. This was a rural community. Residences were split up with acreage and small farms. Another left and they jogged by two houses where she rarely saw people. At the next intersection, she slowed down to pet the donkey that always came over to the fence and brayed for them to stop. This evening was no different. She enjoyed watching Mugshot and the donkey touch noses and stare at each other.

She stopped to pet the donkey's neck while Mugshot and the donkey stared.

A crash and a scream tore through the calm.

Her instinct was to run straight at the sound, but she held back, listening and staring into the growing dusk.

"No! No! Please!" A woman was flung out of the door of the house on this property, not fifty feet from where Dela stood.

She tied Mugshot to the post and ran over to where the woman lay motionless on the ground. She started to kneel but felt a presence. Peering up at the door, an average-sized Indigenous man stood on the threshold.

"Get away from her!" He hopped down the steps.

"Why did you throw her out of the house?" Dela asked, not moving. The unconscious woman needed protection.

"I said get away from her!" the man roared and swung at Dela.

She ducked.

Mugshot started barking. The fence he was tied to creaked.

She took her eyes off the man for a split second, and his fist caught her alongside the head. She stumbled to the side. Her teeth rattled, her ear rang, and shooting stars lighted her vision.

Dela blinked and forced her eyes to focus. The man

drew a foot back, ready to kick the unconscious woman.

Dela grabbed the first thing her hands came upon. A two-by-four. She hit the man as hard as she could, knocking him away from the woman. "Leave her alone! You've done enough damage."

He lay on the ground only a few scconds, before rolling to his feet and charging her. She was forced backward ten steps before losing her balance. Her back hit something that sent shards of pain through her torso. She couldn't give in to the pain. The board was still in her hands. She raised it in both hands, and slammed down on the back of his head.

The man slumped to the ground.

She hobbled over to where Mugshot was howling and jerking on the leash and post. "Shhh, it's okay. I'm okay." She hugged the dog and led him over to the woman. "Down," she told Mugshot, having him lie next to the woman. Then she unhooked the leash and tied the man's hands together behind his back before also tying him to an old axle.

Sitting next to the woman and checking for a pulse, she called the police.

♠ ♣ ♥ ♦

Fifteen minutes later, the woman and man had come to.

"You could be hurt, don't move," Dela told the woman. What's your name?" She wanted to put the woman at ease and give her something to think about rather than her injuries.

"Ina," the woman said in a whisper.

"I'm Dela. Your husband won't hurt you. I have him tied up. Remain still to not worsen your injuries."

The way the woman had been thrown out of the house, she could have spinal injuries.

Dela received permission from the woman to go into the house and get water and a towel to clean up some of her injuries. When the man started yelling how he was going to kill both of them, she shoved a rag in his mouth.

A tribal vehicle pulled in the driveway. The headlights blinded Dela and revealed more damage to the woman than she'd realized.

"Damn Dela, what did you do?" Jacob Red Bear asked as he jogged up to her.

She nodded to the woman, Ina, "I was jogging by when I saw this woman fly out of the door and land here." She went on to tell him how she'd stood between the man and the woman to keep her safe and he'd started beating on her. "He's tied up over there."

Jacob beamed his flashlight in the direction of the man, and Dela tried to ease the woman's fears.

"He's just going to beat me up again when he gets out of jail," Ina said in a whisper. "You should have just let me die. Then I wouldn't feel any more pain."

"No. I'm not about to let him win and neither should you. There are resources to help you. He didn't just beat you. He beat me. That should keep him in jail long enough for you to get started on a new life away from here."

"Where would I go?" the woman whispered.

"We'll figure that out later." Dela pet Mugshot, and said loudly, "She needs the paramedics."

Jacob had the man cuffed, but thankfully, hadn't taken the rag out of his mouth. The man glared at her and the woman on the ground as they walked by.

"He's going to find me and kill me." The woman's body shook.

"I'm going to get a blanket to warm you." Dela entered the house, again. She crossed the room to the couch and grabbed a knitted blanket bunched on the end. Her gaze drifted to a picture frame on the side table. It was of the woman, the man, and a child. Her heart raced. Was there a child in here hurt?

Dela flicked the lights on in all the rooms and looked into the closets. She didn't find a child. With the blanket in her arms, she returned to the woman.

Jacob knelt beside Ina, asking her to tell him what had happened.

Dela spread the blanket over Ina and sat beside Mugshot who remained beside the woman. Petting her dog, Dela listened to Ina's frail voice tell how her husband came home from work upset. He didn't like anything she'd fixed for dinner. Then after throwing the plate of food at her, he put a hand around her throat asking her where she'd sent his boy.

This was good news to Dela. The child wasn't even in the house.

"Where is your boy?" Jacob asked.

The woman barely moved her head. "No. I won't tell you or anyone. He is safe. That is all that matters."

"We're going to make sure you are safe and with your boy," Dela said, studying Jacob.

He raised his gaze to hers and nodded before giving the woman on the ground his full attention. "We will do all we can to keep your husband in jail while you are relocated, if that is what you wish. We can get you a domestic violence advocate who will help you get away and be reunited with your son."

The ambulance arrived. Dela rose slowly, her body ached all over. Mugshot pushed up under her arm, helping her to right herself. "Thanks, boy," she whispered, grasping his collar.

One paramedic conferred with Jacob while the other dropped to his knees beside Ina. Dela stood back, knowing Jacob would need to take her statement. Her jaw and back ached. Glancing around, she noticed two stacked tires. She walked over, holding Mugshot's collar, and sat. Her good leg was shaking.

Jacob, and the paramedic he was talking to, walked over to her.

"I need to take a look at you," the paramedic said, placing a bag beside her. "Sorry about the light." He held a flashlight up to look at her.

Jacob sucked in air. "Dela, what happened to your face?"

She pointed to the tribal vehicle where the man had been stashed. "He clobbered me on the side of the head when I took my eyes off him. I was standing between him and his wife."

"I don't see any cuts, but the swelling and bruising will be there for a while. Did he hit you anywhere else?" The paramedic ran the beam of his light down her arms.

"He shoved me into something pointy over there." She raised the hand not fisted in Mugshot's hair and pointed into the darkness beyond the porch. She'd been beat up a time or two when arresting drunk soldiers, but this time she hadn't had an adrenaline rush or someone backing her up. This time she'd been fighting for her life.

Jacob walked in the direction she'd pointed, his

flashlight lighting the way ahead of him.

"Where did you land?" the paramedic asked.

"My back."

He moved behind her.

Mugshot growled.

"It's okay. He won't hurt me," she told the dog, hugging his neck as the cold air stung her back when the paramedic raised her shirt.

"It looks like a dozen needles poked you. When was your last tetanus shot?"

She heard the zipper on the bag, and said, "I can take care of this."

"No, she can't," Jacob said, standing in front of her. "She lives alone and can't doctor her own back."

She glared up at her friend's brother. He was annoying when he was little and he was even more annoying as an adult. She cursed as the paramedic cleaned the wounds. She didn't know which hurt worse, the initial stabbing or the stinging of the antiseptic.

"It looks like you were shoved against a board with nails sticking out." Jacob handed her the leash she'd used to tie up the man.

"Thanks." She clipped the leash to Mugshot as the paramedic tore tape.

Another car arrived. She glanced toward the lights and didn't think anything of another tribal vehicle arriving.

"What the hell did you do?" Heath's voice jerked her gaze to the tribal officer stalking toward her.

"I tried to keep a husband from killing his wife." She asked over her shoulder, "Could you ask how Ina is doing?"

The paramedic lowered her shirt. "I'll ask. Don't

go anywhere, you still haven't answered my question about a tetanus shot." The man walked away.

"Dela, are you okay?" Heath asked, crouching in front of her.

"I still need to take her statement," Jacob said.

"I'll take it and then I'll take her home," Heath said.

As much as she wanted to object, Dela didn't think she could make it home on her own.

"Works for me. I'll get Ina off to the hospital and take the husband to jail." Jacob put a hand on her shoulder. "What you did was brave and stupid. I'm glad you're okay." He squeezed her shoulder and walked over to where the paramedics were moving Ina onto a gurney.

"You want to give your statement to me after you're home?" Heath asked.

"No. Now, while I still remember it clearly." She wanted to get the statement over with and go home to a long hot shower. She shivered as the night air grew colder.

"How about I take your statement in the house, where it's warmer?" Heath reached out to take her arm.

"No." She stared at his face in the filtered beam of the flashlight. "I can't make it up the steps, again. It's been a while since I've practiced hand-to-hand combat." She smiled even as she chastised herself for not keeping up with her strength training. The first thing tomorrow she was going to order weight equipment to go in her spare bedroom.

"Here." Heath took off his coat and put it around her shoulders. Then he pulled out his logbook and a pen. "Talk fast so I can get you home."

She relayed each event as it happened, from seeing the woman fly out of the door like a rag doll, to her knocking the man out with the two-by-four and tying him up with the dog leash.

Heath leaned back when she'd finished. He stared down at her. "Dela, I know you've been trained to charge in and protect, but you aren't the same person."

She glared at him. "Don't tell me I'm not the same person. I know that. Every waking second of my life, I know I'm not the same. But seventeen years in the army, defending *your* right to do whatever the hell you want to do, is hard to forget. Especially when you see an innocent person being hurt."

"I'm sorry. I didn't mean to sound like—"

"My mother? I moved out of her house because she wouldn't let me forget I'm different. Don't you start up or I'll make sure we don't cross paths." It saddened her to think she may have to avoid the one person who could make her laugh and enjoy life because he considered her damaged goods.

"Hey, I'm just saying, you have to fight smarter and know your limits." He grabbed her arm as the ambulance and tribal vehicle departed. "Come on. You need a hot shower and a cold compress on your face."

"Shouldn't you be off duty by now?" she asked, to change the subject and shoved to her feet.

"I was just getting ready to clock out when I heard the call about a domestic disturbance in Tutuilla and your name mentioned." He led her over to his vehicle, placing her in the front seat and Mugshot in the back.

Chapter Twelve

Mugshot whimpered all the way back to Dela's house and lay outside the bathroom door while she showered.

Dela swung out of her bedroom, still under construction, on her crutches and found Heath stripped down to his t-shirt, uniform slacks, and bare feet in her kitchen, popping popcorn.

"Why are you still here?" she asked, lowering onto the single chair at the card table.

"I wanted to make sure you didn't have any accidents or need anything while you were showering." He turned toward her with a grin on his face. "And I know how much popcorn drizzled with chocolate cheers you up, so…" He placed a bowl of still hot popcorn, adorned with a thin drizzle of melted chocolate, on the table.

"Did you melt my candy bars?" She narrowed her eyes.

"Only one. I'll have my popcorn chocolate-free." He leaned his butt against the counter, then straightened and walked over to her freezer. "I spotted this bag of peas in your freezer. I figured it's here as an ice pack since you don't like peas." He brought the bag over and handed it to her. "Your face could use some ice."

"Thanks." She gingerly touched the cold bag of vegetables to her swollen face. "Ow! That stings." She placed her elbow on the table and leaned her face against the bag while slipping a chocolate-covered piece of popcorn in her mouth. "I could have used your TLC a time or two in the army."

Heath studied her. "How many fights did you get into?"

"Not as many as I could have." She peered up at him. "Thanks for being here. As much as I tell everyone I'm okay, I'm not always okay."

He smiled. "I know. You've always been like that."

Mugshot stood at the door and whined. Before Dela could get her crutches gathered, Heath opened the door and let the dog out.

"Thanks, again."

"No problem. I'd offer to spend the night, but I noticed your bed isn't set up and we wouldn't get any sleep with the two of us on that recliner." He grinned the mischievous grin that had drawn her to him decades ago.

"That's true. Last time I talked to Travis, he said the house should be done by the end of the month. If you're still looking for a place to stay, you're welcome to stay here." When his eyes brightened, she added, "In the larger spare bedroom. The smaller one will be a weight room."

"It's a deal. Want me to stay tonight until you're ready to turn in?"

"No. We're fine now. Thank you for bringing me home, and the popcorn."

He kissed the top of her head. "I'll see you tomorrow."

"Yeah." She remembered Quinn would be there to pick her up at eight. "I don't know if I'll see you tomorrow. Quinn and I are making that trip to Idaho."

Heath crossed his arms. "Call him and tell him you aren't in any shape to chase down leads with him."

"No. You heard Kenny. Bernie expects me to find the killer. Quinn doesn't always pick up on things that aren't said. I need to go." She pushed up off the table and shoved the crutches under her arms. "If I ice my face off and on during the night, I should just have to use makeup to cover the bruising."

Heath shook his head. "You don't have to be so tough."

"It's in my DNA. Go on. Get your shoes and shirt on and go home."

By the time Mugshot woofed at someone approaching the door, Dela had downed four cups of coffee and applied makeup to the side of her face three times, trying to make it look natural. The bags under her eyes didn't help the bad makeup job. She couldn't sleep on her back in the recliner and couldn't find a comfortable position on her side. She'd ended up piling blankets on the floor and sleeping on her stomach the last three hours of the night.

She put Mugshot into the backyard and picked up her purse, opening the door as Quinn stepped on the porch. "I'm ready," she said, stepping forward, trying to get him to take a step back.

"We're in no hurry. I'm here. A tour wouldn't take that long." He stepped around her and entered the house.

Letting out an exasperated sigh, she closed the door and pivoted in time to see the frown on Quinn's face. "I told you it wasn't ready to be seen."

He walked over to a corner of the living room and picked up a cell phone. "You might want this for our trip." His gaze landed on her, and he crossed the room in three long strides. "What happened to your face?"

"I was involved in a domestic dispute last night—"

"Who hit you? Was it Heath? I'll take care of him." The phone in his hand rang. He held it out to her.

Her phone was in her purse. This had to be Heath's. "Hello?" she answered.

"Hey, I did leave my phone there. How are you this morning?" Heath asked.

"I didn't sleep well, and I can't apply makeup. Quinn's here. We're getting ready to head out. What do you want me to do with your phone?" She glanced at the special agent. His face had darkened and was set in a scowl.

"I'll be there in twenty minutes. If you want to leave the door unlocked for that long, I'll grab it and lock it behind me."

"That works." She ended the call and placed the phone on the arm of the recliner where Heath would see it. "Ready?"

"We're not leaving here until you tell me why Seaver's phone was here and you were in a domestic dispute." Quinn crossed his arms and studied her.

"I thought you wanted a tour of the house," she countered, walking into the dining room.

He followed, glancing at the one cup and bowl in the dish drainer.

"I can tell you about my eventful evening while we're driving. What else can we fill up that much time talking about?" She motioned to the kitchen area. "This is the kitchen. The remodel is done on these two rooms and the living room. Travis is still working on the bedrooms and the guest bath."

Quinn headed down the hall.

She didn't want to see his expression when he stared at the handicapped bars in her bathroom. Or what he might have to say about the crutches leaning against the chair where she took her prosthesis on and off. The one made for running was in the closet and she knew the door was closed. She had a thing about no gapping doors or drawers.

He returned to the living room. "Let's go."

She waited for him to walk out of the house, then pulled the door shut, not locking it. If he noticed he didn't say a word.

Dela walked up to the SUV and settled into the passenger seat, keeping her back from touching the seat. She'd ease back and try it out after she became tired of sitting straight. She'd worn her fluffiest sweatshirt to cushion the wounds. The bandage the paramedic had applied came off during the night from her shower and all her wiggling to get comfortable.

Quinn backed up the vehicle and headed to the interstate. "So, what happened last night?"

She relayed about going jogging and getting caught up in a domestic dispute. "Heath was one of the assisting tribals. He took my statement and gave me a ride home. He must have set his phone down and Mugshot's tail caught it, flinging it into the corner." She wasn't going to tell him Heath had made himself comfortable while she showered.

"Why didn't you call for the police instead of jumping in?" Quinn asked.

She stared at him. "You wouldn't have called the police if you saw a body thrown out a door. You would have raced over to see if you could help. It's in us to help first."

"Did the wife-beater hurt you anywhere else?" he asked.

"He shoved me up against a board with nails—"

"When was your last tetanus shot?"

"Sheesh, you're as bad as the paramedic last night. I've only been out of the army for three years and you can be sure when my leg was full of shrapnel that I was given a tetanus shot. I'm good." Memories of the faces of the medical personnel she'd encountered before the actual surgery to remove her leg, flooded her mind. So many concerned faces.

Quinn's deep voice brought her back to the present. "What?" She glanced his direction.

"I asked if there were any children involved."

"I saw a photo of a boy in the house. I hunted for him, fearing he might have tried to come between the husband and wife, but later the woman said he was safe. That was part of what caused her beating. The husband wanted to know where his boy was. She must have left him with someone she trusted to make sure her husband didn't hurt him." Dela's chest expanded with pride, thinking she saved the boy's mother from certain death.

The two would be reunited and the man would never know where they were.

They talked about how to go about questioning Timmons after they passed Baker City. That conversation finished up by the time they were nearing Ontario. Quinn took 95 north. They drove into the small town surrounded by the Weiser River and farm ground.

"Does Timmons live in town?" Dela asked.

"According to the GPS, he has some acreage along the river." Quinn turned on the GPS on his dash and they followed the female voice to a newer home and barn.

As they slowed to park, three medium-sized dogs ran out of the house. Timmons stood holding the door open.

"Did you call and tell him we were coming?" Dela asked.

"No." Quinn slid out of the vehicle as Dela moved to the front to join him. They walked up to the man standing at the door.

"Mr. Timmons, we have some more questions for you," Quinn said.

The man nodded. "I had a feeling I'd have to answer more questions, but I was tired of hanging around that casino. Come on in." He backed up and Quinn entered first.

Dela closed the door behind them.

"This is my wife, Gail." Timmons introduced a plump woman in her forties. The couple stared at Dela's face.

"Sorry. I was breaking up a dispute last night and got caught in the middle." She pointed to her obviously even worse makeup job than she'd thought.

The two nodded and the wife said, "I'll get some coffee going," and walked out of the room.

Timmons walked over to what appeared to be his recliner and sat. "Have a seat. What do you need to know from me?"

"We've discovered that your room had a connecting door with the room where the victim was killed. Did you use that door at any time?" Quinn pulled out his notepad.

Timmons shook his head. "I didn't touch it. I didn't know who was on the other side." A blush added a tint of pink to his cheeks. "I wasn't about to open it and find Connie Oswood on the other side. That woman would have found a way to use my curiosity against me."

"You had her figured out?" Dela asked.

He blinked several times and nodded his head. "She has been at the summits to make sure whoever she's working for has evidence to keep the breaching from happening."

"You're sure of that?" Quinn asked.

"Talk to Ted Barret and Sid Waugh. She bought them drinks and seduced them back to her hotel room, and then the next thing they know she's saying she's going to show photos of them drunk and being unprofessional to their bosses if they don't join the group against breaching the dams." He shook his head as his wife carried in a tray with four cups of coffee and a plate of cookies. "I don't want to lose my job or interfere in the exploration of doing what is right for the fish."

"What time did you go to your room on Wednesday night?" Quinn asked.

"I was up early that morning to drive over and get registered." He glanced at his wife. "What time did I call you? That was after I'd gone to my room for the night."

"It was around nine." She handed everyone a cup of coffee and passed the plate.

Dela's stomach had started growling at Ontario. She plucked two sugar cookies from the plate and nibbled as Quinn did all the questioning. Flipping back through her mind, Dela realized the man was lying. He might have gone to his room at nine, but he'd told them he'd gambled until after midnight when they first talked to him. She cast a glance at the woman avidly listening to the conversation. Perhaps he didn't want his wife to know about his gambling.

"Did you let anyone into your room that night?" Quinn picked up one cookie and balanced it on the edge of his coffee cup.

"No. It was just me." The man bit into a cookie and then sipped his coffee.

"Did you see anyone fighting with Mr. Silva on Wednesday?" Quinn picked his cookie up and took a bite.

"The usual. Not really fighting, just Kevin having to listen to Harvey Beecher and other people against the breaching. But I did see Tommy Darkhorse in Kevin's face. That was unusual, they always looked as if they were friends." Timmons sipped his coffee.

"And you were friends with Kevin Silva?" Quinn asked.

The man paused. "Not friends, but acquaintances. Kevin worked for the largest power company in Idaho. His employers would be out lots of money if we breach the dams. But Kevin was looking at all sides. He actually talked to everyone, one on one, who came to the summits. The last I talked to him, it sounded like he was leaning toward breaching. But then I heard he was discussing other options with a couple of other power company employees who were at the summit. All I want is to help the fish." Timmons downed the rest of his coffee.

"Who do you think would have had reason to kill Kevin?" Dela asked. She wanted to see if the man who had the access to the room without being seen, would point a finger at someone else.

"Honestly, while the topic can cause hot conversations, I can't think of anyone who would stoop so far as to kill the one man who was trying to make it right for everyone." The sorrow on his face wasn't a ploy. The man didn't understand why Kevin was killed.

Chapter Thirteen

"Before we head back to Pendleton, let's stop by and have a chat with Kevin's boss," Quinn said as they drove away from the Timmons's house.

Dela thought that was a good idea. "Did Shaffer actually talk to Steve Wallen?"

"I'm not sure. I do know the agent I sent to talk to him was shuffled off to someone else." Quinn glanced over at her. "That to me means he is avoiding us."

Dela eased back against the car seat and winced.

"What else is hurting that you didn't tell me?" Quinn asked, glancing her way.

"It's just my back. I'm tired of sitting forward, but it hurts to put pressure on the wounds. I'll be fine." She sat sideways, leaning her shoulder into the back of the seat. But that had her staring at Quinn.

"Maybe we should stop somewhere and get some more makeup. The side of your face is turning an ugly blueish-purple."

"I'd rather have that than a crappy makeup job."
She glanced down at her phone and texted Tammie at
the casino security office to see how things were going.
Kenny knew she was on this trip with the FBI Agent
but he had worked last night and wouldn't be there until
tonight's shift.

*Everything is fine. Kenny said you wouldn't be in
and for everyone to do what they normally do.*

Good. Call if anything does come up.

I will.

She smiled. Except for a couple of people she
would like to fire, who were relatives of Casino board
members, she had a good group of people working
security.

"Everything okay at the casino?" Quinn asked.

"Yeah. They can get along without me for a day."

The traffic was heavier as they entered Interstate
84. She sat faced forward and was glad she lived where
she did. If she had to deal with this many cars every
day, she'd go crazy.

When the signs started indicating they were in
Boise, Quinn left the interstate and followed the GPS to
a large building with the power company logo on the
front.

"Let's go find out why Mr. Wallen is avoiding us."
Quinn parked the SUV.

They both exited, walking toward the front of the
building. Inside, they walked over to a podium where a
security guard stood.

Quinn flashed his badge and asked for Mr. Wallen.

The guard picked up a phone and spoke into it. He
listened and put the phone down. "Mr. Wallen is in a
meeting. If you go up the stairs to the left, you can

make an appointment with his secretary."

Quinn nodded to the man and headed to the stairs.

Dela didn't feel like climbing a flight of stairs but didn't want to ask Quinn to find an elevator. She followed the agent's grumbling form up the stairs. He hit the top a good ten stairs before she did.

She stopped at the top to scan the area.

Quinn stood at a reader board on the wall. He walked over to her. "There's a conference room down this way. Let's go see if he's in a conference of just trying to hide from us."

She nodded and walked beside him down the hallway. There was a long glass wall that revealed an elongated conference table and a dozen chairs. There wasn't a soul in the room. They backtracked to the top of the stairs and followed the signage to the CEO's office.

A woman in her forties sat behind a large dark wood desk. She glanced up when they entered. "May I help you?"

Quinn showed his badge. "We're here to talk with Mr. Wallen."

"Your names?"

"Special Agent Quinn Pierce and Head of Security Dela Alvaro."

Dela didn't smile or cringe that the way Quinn said it made her sound like an FBI agent as well.

The woman had written down the titles and names. She picked up the phone. "There are two FBI agents here to talk with you." A pause. "No, I didn't ask them what it was about." She glanced at them. "Mr. Wallen would like to know what this is about?"

Dela didn't wait for Quinn to speak. "It's about a

protest to the dam breaching."

Quinn did a slight head bob as if acknowledging that was the topic.

The secretary relayed that information and they were led to a door down the hall. The woman knocked, waited for a "come in," and opened the door, waving Dela and Quinn on through.

The office was as large as her kitchen, dining room, and living room put together. Two walls were floor-to-ceiling windows overlooking downtown Boise. The park in the background made a tranquil view.

The nameplate at the front of the five-by-eight-foot, dark wood desk said Steve Wallen, CEO. The man stood and stretched a hand across the immaculate desk. Dela wondered if he even did any work other than talk on the phone or go to meetings.

"Agents." He shook first Quinn's hand and then hers before motioning for them to sit in the two chairs in front of his desk. "What's this about a protest?"

Quinn glanced at her, but since she wasn't really an FBI agent, she decided to let him tell the man that wasn't really why they were here.

"Mr. Wallen, we're here to ask you about an employee. Kevin Silva." Quinn waited only long enough for the man to blink and went on. "He was murdered at the casino in Pendleton where he was conducting a summit about whether or not the Snake River dams should be breached."

"Now I thought—" The CEO started.

Quinn barreled on. "We would like to know if he sent you the email threats on his life and if he sent you the report on his findings?"

"I don't have time to deal with this." The man

stretched his hand toward his phone.

"If you call in someone else, I'll have to assume you have something to do with your employee's death." Quinn's gaze and stern demeanor made Dela smile inside.

"You can't come in here and threaten me…" The man's face was red and his eyeballs were nearly popping out of his head.

Dela felt he could fall over from stress-related issues at any moment. "Sir, we know Kevin forwarded the threats he received to you, personally. We found some threatening emails on Kevin's computer. We'd like to take a look at all of them to see if one could be from his killer. And we know he wrote up a recommendation for the breaching of the dams after extensive research and talking with people. We found that on his computer as well. What we want to know is, did you know he was recommending the breaching? And if so, who did you tell?" She could feel Quinn's gaze on her, no doubt, wishing she'd kept her mouth shut. Refusing to give in to his intimidation, she held the CEO's gaze.

Mr. Wallen leaned back in his chair. "He recommended we breach the dams?" The man appeared as if he'd been slugged in the gut. "He told me just last week, he thought we could get by without doing that if we tried something else."

"Can you think of anyone, other than you, who might have received that email?" Quinn asked, pulling out his notepad and pen.

"I'm sure if anyone had received an email with that recommendation, I would have heard about it. We have been scrambling to figure out how to make it right for everyone." The CEO picked up the phone. "Gina, send in Palmer, ASAP." He dropped the phone back on the cradle and stared over their heads as his right pointer finger tapped on the desk.

The door opened. An average-sized man with a bald head rushed in. He stopped as soon as he spotted Dela and Quinn.

"Palmer, did you get an email from Kevin saying we needed to breach the dams?" Wallen glared at the man.

Dela felt sorry for Palmer. He'd been summoned here as if there was a crisis and then asked a question, she was sure he knew his boss didn't want to hear the answer.

"No. As far as I know, Kevin hasn't contacted anyone here since he left for Pendleton." Palmer glanced at both she and Quinn.

"You say that like you don't know he's dead," Dela said.

Palmer's gaze nailed her to the chair. "He's what?"

"It appears your boss doesn't keep you in the loop," Quinn said. He stood and introduced himself and Dela. "Were here to see the email threats Kevin received and find out who he'd sent an email to about the dam breaching."

Palmer flicked a glance at Wallen. "I don't know anything about any of that."

Quinn faced the CEO. "We'd like to talk to all of the employees in this building. Can you round them up and have them come to the conference room we saw down the other hallway?"

"Why should I do that?" Wallen groused.

"Because if you don't, it looks like you are

covering up a homicide…"

Palmer gasped.

"And that means you are an accessory." Quinn slipped his notepad back in his jacket pocket.

Dela stood, emphasizing they meant business.

Wallen waved a hand. "Palmer, do whatever they ask. Just all of you get out of my office."

Dela and Quinn exchanged a glance and followed Palmer out into the hall.

"Do you really want to talk to everyone in the building?" the man asked, stopping halfway down the hall between the boss and his secretary.

"No. We want to learn more from you and anyone else here who might know something about the threats and the email." Quinn nodded that they keep on moving.

Palmer started to say something and Quinn cut him off, "Let's wait until we're in the conference room."

Palmer shook his head. "We need to meet in the cafeteria or outside."

Dela studied the man. He knew something about the conference room. There was a reason the CEO didn't mind them speaking to his employees in that room.

Quinn led them down the stairs and out to an area with a couple of cement picnic tables and benches.

Dela sat on one of the benches. Quinn joined her. Palmer stood, pacing.

Quinn pulled out his notepad. "Why do you think your boss didn't tell you about Silva's death?"

Palmer stopped and stared at them. "I can't believe he's dead. He was the best man for his job. He knew how to keep people calm and still get his point across."

"Why didn't Wallen want you to know the man was dead?" Dela asked.

"Probably because I would quit. And I will now that I know. Wallen has had us changing the reports to favor leaving the dams in. Kevin is the only one who would stand up to him and show him the true facts." Palmer ran a hand over his bald head. "I can tell you, Wallen didn't like Kevin. He called him a Do-gooder behind his back. Also made some racial slurs about Mrs. Silva."

Quinn closed his notepad. "Can you send me all the threats that were sent to Wallen from Kevin?"

The man shook his head. "I can't. But I'll talk to Joyce. She's in tech. She might be able to."

"Can she also see if Kevin sent an email to Wallen Thursday morning sometime between one and three a.m.?" Dela asked.

"I'll see what I can do. Do you really think Wallen had something to do with Kevin's death?" Palmer's bottom lip quivered a little and his eyes flicked back and forth as if he feared everything around him.

"We won't know for sure until we see what he's hiding." Quinn stood. "If Wallen asks, tell him we were called away on another pressing case."

Palmer nodded.

"And here's my card. Have Joyce forward all the information to me at the email on this." Quinn handed the man his card.

"Am I in danger?" Palmer asked.

"Not if you just say what I told you and not let him know you talked to Joyce." Quinn stared at the man. "Can you do that?"

"I'll try."

Dela smiled at the man. "If you were a friend of Kevin's, you can do it for his sake."

The man nodded.

Quinn pulled out his phone and walked away.

Dela followed. "Are we headed home?" she asked, climbing into the SUV.

"Yes. I'll have local agents keep tabs on Wallen and Palmer." Quinn started up the vehicle and drove out of the parking lot. "Hungry?"

"Yes."

"We'll grab something to eat and then head back." Quinn wound his way up and down streets before pulling into a parking spot near an Italian restaurant. "Will this work?"

Dela's stomach did a dance. It had been a while since she'd had good Italian food. "It will do." She didn't want Quinn to know how much she liked this cuisine.

Entering the restaurant there were only a few tables with patrons. It was the middle of the afternoon. She was surprised the establishment was open.

After they were seated and given salads and a bread basket, Dela relaxed, enjoying the food.

"What did you think of Wallen?" Quinn asked, picking up his water glass.

"He's hiding something. Whether it's Kevin's death or something else, it's too soon to tell." She bit off the end of her second breadstick.

"That's what I thought. Why didn't he tell the other employees about Silva's death? That seems off. And the way Palmer acted as if everything in that building was overheard…"

"Yeah, that sends up red flags." Dela leaned back

as the waitress arrived with their large round platters of food.

Just the aroma of the tomato sauce made her mouth start watering. She really needed to eat out more.

They savored their food for a couple of minutes before Quinn picked up his glass of water, drank, set the glass back down, and studied her.

The food in Dela's mouth didn't taste as good as before the man across from her stopped eating.

"What is really going on between you and Seaver?" Quinn asked.

Dela swallowed the bite in her mouth, picked up her water, and drank. When a quarter of the cup was empty, she eased her back against the chair. "The only thing going on between us is friendship. I hadn't realized how much I'd missed having a friend who knew everything about me and who I didn't have to pretend I was okay around."

Quinn picked up his fork and slowly rolled a noodle around the tines. "Pretend? I've never known you to do anything but show your true self."

She shook her head. "See, that's where you don't know me. There's stuff in my past that nags and eats at me every day. Stuff that only Heath knows and understands."

"Okay, I understand that. I've got a buddy who knows all my demons. But we only connect when those demons surface unbidden."

Dela stared at Quinn. "We haven't seen one another or had any contact since I entered the army. He sent me a couple of letters but I ignored them. I went into the army to put my past behind me." She laughed sarcastically. "Funny thing is, I couldn't get away from it. If I wasn't busy, it would consume me worse there than at the rez." She smiled. "Seeing Heath step out of that room the other morning, it was like I'd found the piece of me that had been missing for a long time. My fun side." She picked up her fork. "So don't lecture me on spending too much time with him or whatever you were planning to do." Dela shoved a forkful of spicy sausage and tomato sauce in her mouth and chewed.

Quinn studied her a few seconds more and began eating.

The special agent didn't know it, but his question made her realize, Heath was exactly what she needed right now. Fun with no attachments. She had a feeling he could help her find out more about her father and help her come to terms with her less-than-perfect body.

Chapter Fourteen

As they pulled into the Casino parking lot, Quinn's phone rang. He parked, looked at his phone, and smiled. "Palmer came through. I have an email from an account at the power company."

Dela smiled. She had a feeling the bald-headed man had more spirit than he'd shown. "Good. Anything interesting?"

Quinn slid his finger across the screen, pressed his thumb on it, and waited. "Hopefully." He began scanning the email.

"I'm going in to check on things. You can come let me know what you've found." She opened the door and slid out.

"There are forty threatening emails. I'll forward this to Shaffer and have him pull out the ones we don't already have." As his fingers moved over his phone, she closed the door and walked into the casino.

She would have rather gone home and changed. A

sweatshirt and jeans weren't her usual work attire. She nodded to two of her security personnel on the floor and headed to the office.

"From the looks of you, you should be home nursing that face. Are you on duty or just checking in?" Tammie asked when Dela entered the security office.

"I wish. I can't rest with a murder linked to the casino. Special Agent Pierce didn't take me home after our trip to talk to the victim's employer. Guess I'll be working incognito today." She walked over to her desk, dropped her purse in a drawer, and picked up the earbuds, radio, and mic. Once the earbuds were in her ears, the radio hooked on her belt, and the mic clipped to her shirt's left shoulder, she checked in with each lead security guard. Everything was running smoothly. Ending her conversation with the last lead, Quinn walked through the door.

"Silva did send his proposal about breaching the dams to Wallen. From what the tech could tell, it had been read/opened as soon as it arrived in Wallen's inbox."

"Which means he'd been waiting for the email. But why couldn't you find where it had been sent on Silva's computer?" Dela asked.

"I have Shaffer looking into that. What it does mean, Wallen knew what Silva was going to say at the summit. I bet he had someone already planted here to make sure Silva sided with the power company." Quinn walked toward the small interview room. "Let's take another look at the backgrounds of the summit attendees."

"Are the records in there?" Dela asked, wondering when her interview room had become an FBI office.

Quinn showed her the laptop bag in his left hand. "They are in the documents for this case."

She sighed. Reading files on a computer didn't seem like a two-person job. "You go ahead and read through them. I need to deal with casino stuff."

He studied her a moment, then entered the room.

Tammie let out a disgusted sound. "You're just going to let him take over that room?"

Dela smiled at her employee. "I'd rather he sit in there alone than me have to be cooped up with him. I've had enough of the FBI man for one day. I'll be over at surveillance if anyone is looking for me."

Tammie gave her a finger wave.

Exiting the security office onto the casino floor, Dela breathed in. She didn't like the acrid scent of cigarette smoke, but she did get a thrill at the sound and activity that met her.

Tapping her security card on the surveillance keypad, she entered.

"Hey, shouldn't you be home taking care of yourself?" Lionel, a man old enough to be her grandfather, asked.

"I wish. No rest when there's been a murder here." Dela continued across the room to Marty's office.

"Your bruises have anything to do with the murder?" Mary asked.

"No. Unrelated incident."

"She saved my cousin from being killed by her husband," a woman's voice said.

Dela stopped at the door and swung around. She scanned the four people on duty. Her gaze landed on Jacee Bing. She was a recent hire. "Are you related to Ina?"

The woman nodded.

"Is it true her son is safe?" Dela had been worried that the husband would go after the son when he made bail.

The fortyish woman smiled and nodded. "None of us know where he is, but Ina said he is safe from Paul. Thank you for saving her. She was ready to give her life to keep her son safe."

Dela didn't handle gratitude well. She always did what was needed and didn't feel there was a need to be thanked. She nodded and ducked into Marty's office.

"Hey, I hear you're a hero," Marty said, swiveling his chair in her direction. When his gaze landed on her face, he closed his mouth.

Her glare had done the trick. "Any chance you've figured out how someone managed to get into Silva's room and strangle him without cameras seeing him?" She held up a hand. "And please don't tell me the cameras had been tampered with." That was the case when they were trying to catch a human trafficker and the last suspect of a murder that happened at the casino.

"This time no cameras were tampered with. I've been going back through each camera that night. So far nothing is popping out at me." Marty shrugged. "You finding anything of interest?"

"FBI Agent Pierce believes the head of the power company had him killed because he was going to give a speech in favor of breaching the dams the next day. The victim had sent an email to the CEO the night he was killed."

Marty leaned back in his chair. "That would mean there was already someone here to take care of things."

"Yeah. Have you noticed anyone lingering on the

sidelines during the summit?"

"No. But I'll bring in Farley and have him start watching the camera footage at the event center."

"That's a good idea. No sense wearing your eyes out when you have someone to help now." Dela nodded toward the monitor. "If either of you sees something, call me first."

Marty grinned. "Always."

She returned the grin and left the office. On her way through the monitor room, she spotted Heath walking into the casino. He carried a file folder in his hand.

Dela hurried out onto the casino floor and intercepted him before he entered the security office. "Hey, how did you know we were back?"

Heath stopped, scanning her face. "I called to tell Pierce we had some more forensics reports. He told me to bring them here. You on duty or off?"

"On. Quinn didn't take me home so I could get into my uniform." She nodded toward the offices. "I guess he told you to bring him the information to the security offices?"

Heath grinned. "Yeah. Has he taken over your job?"

"No, just my space. We need to get this thing solved and get him out of here." She continued to the security office and shoved the door open.

Tammie smiled as they walked side by side over to the interview room door.

Dela shoved it open and found Quinn hunched over the laptop, reading. "Found Heath headed this direction," she said.

Quinn slowly turned, his gaze landing on the man

standing beside her. "Seaver." The agent held out his hand and Heath handed him the folder.

Dela frowned. Why was Heath bowing to Quinn's alphabet position?

"Did you see anything interesting in these?" Quinn asked.

Heath pulled a chair out on the other side of the table and sat. He motioned for Dela to join them.

Like she was going to walk away after delivering him and the folder. She sat, now unsure of which man she was more irritated with.

"The only fingerprints on the lamp were those of the last person to clean the room." Heath glanced her direction. "The woman who found the body."

Dela knew Rae. She was a woman who had worked in housekeeping for nearly ten years. There wasn't any reason to believe she had touched the lamp other than when cleaning the room. She nodded.

"They did find several different types and colors of hair. Several long dark hairs could have been from Mrs. Silva, or they could be from when Tommy Darkhorse visited the victim. There was also hair from the victim and long bleached blonde strands."

Dela sat up straight. "Like would match Connie Oswood?" They hadn't seen the woman go into the room. But if her hair was in the room, she had to have found a way in.

"We'll know for sure when forensics gets done running the DNA on them. They said most of the hairs had follicles intact." Heath pulled out another piece of paper. "We discovered that your Ms. Oswood has been connected with three other struggles between energy companies and Native American tribes."

Dela plucked the page from his hands and started reading.

"What do you mean?" Quinn asked, taking the page from Dela.

She glared at him and waited for Heath to fill them in.

"It appears she is a corporate 'helper.' She appears at events being held by the entities against, say, a fuel line being laid across a reservation or as with this, a power company not wanting their dam breached. She pays or persuades people to vote the way of the energy company. She's paid big money to make problems go away."

"You think she was paid to make Silva go away?" Quinn asked.

"I think she is our best suspect," Heath said, glancing at Dela.

She couldn't hide the smile on her face. She'd known the woman was up to something from the first time they'd met. "I like her for it. But how did she get into the room without being seen?"

Dela snapped her fingers. "She was being friendly with Beecher. And her room was on the other side of Beecher's. She could have used the connecting door to get into his room." Her heart raced thinking she'd found the way Connie entered the room.

"They might have had a connecting door, but how did she get into the victim's room? Was it connected to the room on the other side?" Heath studied her.

Dela stood. "Let's go take a look at the murder scene."

The two men exchanged glances and followed her out of the security offices and over to the elevator.

Rosie "yoo-hooed" and waved. Dela smiled but didn't waver from her path to prove Ms. Oswood killed Mr. Silva.

She pressed the elevator button. The two men caught up to her by the time the elevator arrived and the doors swished open. A couple and a middle-aged man exited. Dela stepped in, standing in front of the panel of buttons. When Quinn and Heath were inside, she hit the button for the tenth floor and stood staring at the panel until the conveyance bounced to a stop and the doors opened. She walked down to room 1020, used her security pass to unlock the door, and entered. Not looking right or left, she walked over to the sliding glass door and out onto the small balcony.

"Like this." She put her hands on the railing and started to swing a leg over.

Hands grabbed her. Both men each had one of her arms.

"We see where you're going with this. You don't have to demonstrate," Heath said, releasing her arm first.

She glared at Quinn who dropped his hold.

"Connie and Beecher could have been working together. He let her into his room, she shimmied over to this balcony and sauntered into the room."

"Wouldn't there have been a struggle?" Quinn asked.

She studied him. "What did you think the first time you saw her?"

He started to open his mouth.

"Honestly, as a man and not an FBI agent? What would be your first reaction if you saw her strutting into your room from the balcony?" She glanced at Heath.

"Either one of you. If a woman that looked and dressed like Connie Oswood sauntered into your hotel room would you be worried she was going to kill you? Especially, if you'd been spurning her advances for weeks and your wife had left because she thought you had been lying to her?"

Both their faces reddened and their eyes darkened before they both nodded slightly.

"Maybe she just said she wanted to share a nightcap with him. She could have poured him a drink, further exploiting she was there to make him happy rather than kill him. She moves behind him, maybe massaging his shoulders, then grabs the closest thing, the lamp cord, and with a bit of a struggle, he's dead." She found this scenario logical.

"But there wasn't a struggle according to forensics," Heath said, ruining her story.

"Maybe she drugged him. Put something in the drink?" She could see the woman doing that to make it easier to do the killing.

"We didn't find evidence of more than one glass," Quinn said.

"She could have taken the glass with the drug with her when she went back into Beecher's room. We need to see if he'll talk." Dela walked through the open door and into the room.

"Beecher checked out this morning. To speak with him will mean another trip to Idaho," Quinn said.

"Did everyone leave? Even Connie Oswood?" she asked.

"Yes, everyone left. We'll have to run all over to talk with them," Quinn said.

She didn't like the idea of driving all over Oregon,

Washington, and Idaho questioning people. That many long trips with Quinn didn't sound appealing.

"I'll see if an agent near Beecher can talk to him about whether or not Ms. Oswood was in his room or if they used the connecting door between their rooms at all." Quinn pulled out his phone and walked out the door into the hallway.

Dela glanced at Heath. "Do you think she climbed across the balconies to get in here?"

"I think there should be fingerprints that would show if she did. I'll see if I can get forensics to check on those." Heath pulled out his phone and walked out into the hallway.

Dela walked over and closed the sliding door. She stared at the RV parking lot down below and then up at the Blue Mountains in the distance and Wildhorse Mountain. She wondered if the victim had talked to his wife about his CEO or any of the other employees at the power company.

Chapter Fifteen

Dela caught up to Heath. "Can you give me a ride to my house? I want to get my car."

"Sure. I delivered the forensic reports to Pierce. Want to go now?" Heath fell in step beside her as they walked toward the elevator.

Quinn stood at the door talking on the phone.

"I have to grab my purse out of the office. I'll meet you at the entrance." She didn't want Quinn saying he'd take her home. She didn't plan on him going with her to talk to Stacy Silva. Dela walked by the elevator and down the hall to the service elevator by the housekeeping room.

Stepping into the service elevator, she relaxed. The sooner this murder was solved the sooner her life could get back to normal. She didn't like having to follow Quinn around or feeling like the rope between two tug of war teams. Neither one had the right to think she was their possession. She wasn't anyone's possession.

In the security office, she let Tammie know she'd be gone for a couple of hours. "I'll be back by nine at the latest. Let Kenny know."

"I will. Enjoy your dinner."

Dela didn't say otherwise. It was that time of day.

She joined Heath at the casino entrance. He had two hotdogs in his hands. He held one out to her.

"I don't like eating alone," he said, as they exited the building.

"I had planned to grab something at home, but thanks." She bit into the end of the dog hanging out of the bun and chewed. There was nothing like the plump hotdogs the deli made, smothered with relish and mustard. It appeared Heath had remembered many things from their time together in high school.

"You going to stay home and rest?" he asked, opening his passenger side door for her.

While on the inside, she thought it was sweet he held the door for her, on the outside, she wasn't about to let him know that little action had affected her. Dela lowered into the tribal car, not rubbing her back against the seat. She finished eating her hot dog as Heath started the car, called in he was off on a break, and pulled out of the parking lot.

"How did the trip to Cambridge go this morning?" he asked, taking a bite of his hot dog.

"Quinn and I both got the feeling the CEO is up to his colored hair in stopping the breaching." As the words came out, she realized what had appeared 'off' with the man. His hair color had been too dark for his pasty complexion.

"Why do you say that?"

She went on to tell him what they'd learned from

Palmer and the information that had been sent to Quinn from a tech at the company. "I'm going to see Stacy Silva at the Rose's. I want to ask her about her husband's boss. Palmer didn't have very good things to say about the man."

Heath parked on the road in front of her house. The short driveway to her garage had two small-sized pickups and Travis's large pickup blocking the way.

"Looks like my remodeling crew is here." She hadn't talked to Travis in a couple of days. It would be good to get caught up with how things were coming along. Dela opened the door and started up the driveway. The clomp of a wooden cowboy heel behind her had her spinning toward the sound.

Heath caught her as her prosthetic foot didn't pivot like a normal foot and she started to topple forward. "Hey. Why are you so jumpy?" He stared into her eyes.

"I'm not. I just thought you were dropping me off and going." Her gaze traveled to his car sitting on the side of the road.

"Thought I'd come in and check out these workers that you leave alone here all day." He was acting like a cop. His eyes were locked on something over her shoulder.

"Travis, Molly's son, is my contractor. He pulled in two of his friends. So far, I can't complain about the work. It's a little slower than someone with more experience, but the price is right and they do really care about quality." She leaned out of his hands and headed to her front door.

Five feet from the door, it opened. Travis's smiling face always put her in a good mood.

"How's my house coming along?" she asked,

entering the living room.

When Travis didn't reply, she glanced over her shoulder, Heath and Travis were giving each other the once over.

"Travis Taylor, this is Heath Seaver. Heath, Travis. Shake hands and let's get on with my tour." She grinned as the two shook hands but didn't say anything.

Travis walked over to her and whispered, "You're not in trouble, are you?"

Dela laughed. "No. Heath is an old friend. I went somewhere with the FBI agent this morning and Heath gave me a ride home to get my car."

Her contractor nodded and headed down the hall. "We finished the guest bathroom and your bedroom today. You can move into it whenever you want. Mom said to tell you she has an extra bed you can borrow until you get one, if you want."

They walked into the smaller of the two guest bedrooms. "We reinforced this wall for exercise equipment to be attached to it and put in a heavier beam up there to hang a punching bag from. Basically, other than paint, this room is done." Travis scowled at Heath standing inside the door of the room.

"I'll go to the hardware store tomorrow and get the paint if you and your crew don't mind painting it." Dela had never had the patience to paint.

"Sure. Toby likes painting better than hammering and measuring." Travis grinned. "He's putting the last coat on the other room."

They filed out of the smallest bedroom and entered the larger guest room. She'd picked a light blue-gray for this room. Until Heath had shown up, she'd planned to make it into her office.

"Nice color," Heath said, smiling.

Dela studied the tall lean Umatilla man in his twenties, moving a paintbrush up and down the wall. He turned from applying two strokes of color in a corner. He had a long narrow face and hair pulled back in a ponytail at the base of his neck.

"Dela picked out all nice colors," Toby said. "It is a pleasure staring at the colors all day."

"You should start a painting company," Dela said, walking over to the young man. "You do beautiful work."

Toby grinned, showing off crooked teeth. "Thank you. It is relaxing." He glanced over her shoulder to Travis. "I hope you like what I did in your room." The young man appeared happy but unsure if she'd like what he'd done.

"I'm sure I will." As they left this room to cross the hall to her bedroom, Dela girded herself to not show anything other than pleasure at whatever Toby had painted in her room.

Travis stood in front of her door. "You were right about Toby getting his own painting company." He opened the door and stepped back.

Dela's gaze landed on the wall opposite where the bed would sit. A tear came to her eye as she took in the sun peeking over a tree-covered mountain. The mural wasn't detailed but rather abstract, blended, and beautiful. "I love it! Toby, you are an artist!"

Heath touched her shoulder and indicated the wall where her bed would sit.

Dela turned and grinned. On the wall near the top, a painted dreamcatcher hung. Five feathers were painted on the wall on either side of the dreamcatcher.

"This is gorgeous. I'll close my eyes at night seeing this serene image and know that I'll not have bad dreams because of the dreamcatcher." She felt tears coming and quickly walked into the bathroom to keep anyone from seeing them.

She heard voices in the other room but used the alone time to compose herself. Purchasing this house had been a spur-of-the-moment idea, but now, she was so glad she had. And that she'd had confidence in her friend's twenty-year-old son and his friends to do the work.

Heath walked in. "You were smart to choose young men who have something to prove to do your remodel."

She nodded, feeling the tears well up. She swiped at her eyes with the sleeve of her sweatshirt. "I don't know how Toby knew that was what I needed in my bedroom. It—" Dela couldn't put her emotions into words.

"He is a perceptive young man." Heath put his arms around her, holding her. "When I move in, you can tell me about the demons that keep you up at night."

She nodded slightly. Of everyone she knew, he would be the one she could tell them to and not feel weak.

"Hey! Oh sorry!" Travis's voice held surprise.

Dela pushed out of Heath's arms. "It's okay. What did you need?" She faced her friend's son and knew Molly would be on the phone asking her about the man her son found holding her.

"Toby's done with the guest room. We're going to call it a night. All that's left is cleaning up and painting the exercise room. We'll do that on Monday."

"Sounds like a plan. I'll take a day and look for furniture. Would you and your crew be willing to haul it and help me put it in the house?"

Travis grinned. "Sure! Can we have people we talk to about remodeling call you?"

"Of course! I would recommend your team to anyone who wants a wonderful remodel." She smiled. "Leave a bill for the rest of what I owe you when you come on Monday."

"I can do that. Thanks." He glanced at Heath. "Nice to meet you." Travis no longer looked at the tribal police officer as if he were the enemy, but he still had a hint of wariness in his eyes.

"Likewise. Tell your mom, 'Hi,' from Heath."

Travis glanced at Dela and then back at Heath. "Okay…"

Toby, Travis, and Melvin, the other young man who worked on her house, walked out the front door. Their vehicles started up and Mugshot woofed at the French door in the dining room.

Dela walked over, opened the door far enough the dog could poke his head in and she scratched his ears and wide forehead, before opening the door all the way. Her large dog walked over, sniffed Heath, and lay down on his bed by the recliner.

"Don't you need to get back to work?" Dela asked.

"Actually, by the time I call in, I'll be off duty. I can hang around and help you with whatever you might need help with." He set the hat he'd been carrying on the card table.

It was growing dark. As much as she wanted to talk with Stacy Silva, it would be close to eight by the time she arrived at the Rose home. The best thing to do would be to put on her uniform and go to work for a few hours and try to talk with Stacy in the morning.

"It's too late to pay a call on the victim's wife. Guess I'll go put in a few more hours at the casino."

Heath shook his head. "You were attacked last night and hauled away from here early this morning. The best thing for you to do is have a calm quiet night at home." He put his hands on her shoulders. "Go take a shower and put your pajamas on. I'll see if I can find something worth watching on the television."

She peered into his eyes. If her mother had told her to take a shower and ignore work, she would have bristled. Heath wasn't her mother. Dela shrugged. She didn't feel like going back to work and she did feel like her body needed to heal. Her ordeal with her leg had taught her how to listen to her body.

"Okay."

Surprise sprang into Heath's dark eyes. "Really? You'll listen to reason?"

"No, I'm listening to my body. It says I need to rest."

"Good. Go take a shower." He walked into the living room and the television came on.

Dela's phone rang. A glance at the name and she groaned. It didn't take long for Travis to tell his mom who had been holding Dela.

She grabbed the phone and headed to her bedroom. This was a conversation she didn't want the man in the living room to hear.

Chapter Sixteen

After she and Heath had watched *Die Hard 2*, he'd left and she'd doubled all the blankets she owned, piling them on her bedroom floor. After dragging Mugshot's bed into the room, they settled down for a mostly restful night.

Sleeping on her stomach had never been one of Dela's favorite sleeping positions but with her back still tender, it was her only option when her hips ached from the plywood under the blankets. While Travis had said her remodel was complete, she still needed to get someone in to put down flooring. She planned on planking throughout the house. It was the easiest to navigate with her crutches.

Dela checked in with the casino Sunday morning close to nine.

Listening to Margie's rundown of the night before at the casino, she nodded her head. It sounded like a normal Saturday. Dela told Margie she'd be in at noon.

She glanced at Mugshot sitting by her chair as she finished up breakfast. "Want to go for a ride with me?"

She'd never had a dog of her own before. And while Mugshot was a lot bigger than any dog she'd ever seen, he had, in the last few months, become important in her life.

The animal stared at her with his big brown eyes and his ears perked up at the sound of her voice. She figured other than his ride home with the person who owned him before, his trip to the vet and then to here were the only times he'd been in a car. And while he'd been fine the two times she'd hauled him, she had to remember, he had a crushed leg the first time and was on pain medication the second time.

"How about we see how well you can get in my car and take it from there?" She picked up her dishes, put them in the sink, and grabbed her purse and car keys from the TV tray by the door. Staring at the tray table, she determined tomorrow she would order her flooring and get it installed as soon as she could. She was ready for furniture.

"Come on."

Mugshot sat down by the door.

She patted her leg. "Come on. We're going for a ride."

The dog continued to sit. She knew he had gone in and out of this door. It was the door they used when they went on walks. That's when she noticed his gaze on the leash hanging from a nail by the door.

"You think you need your leash. Okay, if that makes you feel safe." She grabbed the leash and the dog stood on his three legs, his tongue hanging out in happiness. Dela led him over to the car and opened the back door. He hopped in and sat in the middle of the seat.

"Now you behave while I'm driving," she said, closing the back door and sliding into the driver's seat.

She backed out of the driveway and headed toward the interstate, crossing over it and past the casino. Wildhorse Mountain was their destination. She wanted to visit with Stacy about her husband's boss.

Dela glanced in the rearview mirror every ten or fifteen minutes to make sure Mugshot wasn't becoming agitated. After thirty minutes, he lowered his body and was soon snoring in the back seat.

Smiling as she listened to the dog's snores, Dela was glad she'd taken this animal into her home. He gave her companionship and didn't ask for anything more than food and a warm bed.

At the Rose home, she noticed the Camaro wasn't visible. There was a rundown shed that it could have been parked in.

"You stay." She rolled the two back windows down about three inches and exited the vehicle. Walking up to the door, she breathed in the pine and musty fall scents that she loved in the mountains.

She knocked twice before the door opened.

Melba Rose stood on the other side of the screen. "Hello? What can I do for you?" she asked.

"Mrs. Rose, I'm Dela Alvaro. I was here the other day with the FBI agent. I wanted to ask Stacy a couple of questions about the man her husband worked for."

"Oh, Stacy's not here. Ben took her home this morning. She wanted to get home to take care of putting her husband in the ground." The woman didn't look the least bit sad.

"Oh, I'm sorry I missed her. If she happens to call after she arrives home, would you have her call me?" Dela pulled a piece of paper out of her purse and wrote her name and phone number on it.

"I'll put it by the phone so I don't forget." The old woman closed the door and disappeared.

Dela headed back to her car.

At the sound of her steps crunching on pinecones, Mugshot barked and sat up. When he saw her, his mouth opened and his tail swung back and forth.

"How about we pull off about a mile from here and take a short walk through the woods." Dela had taken a walk on the mountains every day after she'd returned home. Each day she'd pushed herself a little further to see how much she could endure and to gain her strength back. Since taking the job at the casino, she'd stopped going.

About two miles from the Rose residence, she pulled the car over on a wide spot in the road and got out. She inhaled, stretched her arms wide, and opened Mugshot's door. He lumbered out, waited for her to grasp his leash, and they walked into the trees and underbrush enjoying nature and a feeling of contentment.

♠ ♣ ♥ ♦

After dropping off Mugshot, Dela went to the casino and fielded her usual Sunday paperwork and a call from Heath asking if she'd slept well.

Three in the afternoon, her phone rang. A glance revealed a number she didn't know.

"Hello?" she answered.

"This is Stacy Silva. Melba said you were out to see me this morning. I'm sorry I wasn't there. I told the tribal police I was going home. I didn't realize they didn't stay in touch with you."

"That's fine. No, they rarely tell me anything. I was wondering, did your husband ever say anything about his boss, Mr. Wallen?"

There was a deep sigh. "Yes. He's not a very nice man. He hasn't even called me. You would think if one of his employees was killed while doing business, he would reach out to the family."

Dela agreed. "Did Kevin have arguments with Mr. Wallen?"

"Not really arguments. Mr. Wallen tried to get Kevin to change the findings when they were leaning toward breaching being better for the fish. Kevin refused and told the people in his division to only use the truth when putting together the charts and information."

That confirmed what Palmer had said. "If Wallen didn't want the truth, why didn't he hire someone who would do what he wanted?"

"Because Kevin had been working as the liaison between the power company and environmentalists and the Indigenous people for ten years. He'd built up a reputation of listening and making informed decisions. That's why I couldn't believe he was going to side with the power company." She choked and sniffled.

"He wasn't siding with the power company. Kevin sent an email to his boss the night he died stating breaching the dams was the only way to save the fish. And he planned to say that at the summit the next day."

"Oh no! If I hadn't been so quick to believe what someone said and not my husband, I would have been with him. He wouldn't have been alone and easy to kill." Sobs echoed through the phone.

Dela heard someone on the other side murmuring to the woman. She waited about three minutes then said, "Hello, I have one more question."

"Yes," Stacy croaked.

"Who did Kevin work the closest with at the power company?"

"Dan Germaine. They were both for breaching the dams."

Dela hadn't expected any name other than Palmer. "What about a Mr. Palmer?"

A harsh laugh barked through the phone. "Stan Palmer? He wanted Kevin's job. Kevin would come home and tell me about how Stan had tried to undermine him."

Dela wrote down Palmer and circled the name. Then Dan Germaine, a dash, and call. "Thank you. Your information has been helpful."

"Call if you have any more questions. I want whoever killed my husband to pay." The line went quiet.

Dela dialed Quinn.

"I didn't expect to hear from you today," Quinn answered.

"Why not? There is still a murder to solve." She tapped her pen on the pad she'd written the information on. "I just talked with Stacy Silva." Dela relayed what she'd learned from the wife of the victim.

"That's interesting. Palmer gave us information that points a finger at Wallen. If he wanted Kevin's job, you would have thought he would have lain all the blame on him, not his boss."

"I was wondering the same thing. I think you need

to call Germaine and see what he has to say about Palmer and Wallen. Stacy said Wallen wasn't a nice man but didn't go into any details." Dela had a question from one of her security guards in the earbud in her ear. "Just a minute.

"Ross, repeat what you asked, please."

"There's a guy down here in the bar and grill that's drunk. But he has his legs wrapped around the table leg. I don't want to get too forceful if you can talk him into releasing the table."

"I'm headed your way." Into her phone, she said, "I have to go help with an altercation. Call Germaine and call me back with what you learn." Dela headed out of the security office, across the casino floor that was quiet for a Sunday afternoon, and into the Pony Bar and Grill.

She spotted Ross and a man in his twenties with his chin on one of the taller tables. A glance under the table and she caught sight of his long legs wrapped around the table leg and his feet hooked together.

Dela walked up. "Can't you find a better dance partner than the table?"

The man's head turned her direction and his dilated eyes bounced in their sockets.

Dela whispered to Ross, "They didn't serve him alcohol, did they?"

"No. Dexter said the man came in looking high, asked for a glass of water, then started yelling and wrapped his legs around the table."

She nodded. "Hey, you look like someone who could use a friend. Can I help you?" Dela pulled out one of the chairs at the table and sat down.

The man's eyes wobbled around as he studied her.

"They can't take me. I know too much."

"We won't let anyone take you. If you could describe who you're afraid of, we can keep an eye out and not let them enter the casino." She kept her voice loud enough he could hear through whatever was going on in his head, but not enough to get the people drinking wound up.

The man shook his head. "Can't describe them. They change."

She tried a different approach. "You can let go of the table. We won't let anyone take you, so you can relax. I'm sure your legs are getting tired of being wrapped around that table leg."

He glanced down and stared at his legs as if he didn't realize he had the table in a headlock. Slowly his foot twisted and his legs sprung from around the leg.

Dela saw Ross start toward the table and shook her head. If they could get him out of here in a calm fashion that would be better P.R.

"I'm Dela. What's your name?" she asked, reaching across the table to shake hands.

The man rubbed his hands together and stared at her hand. "Rudy."

"Rudy, have you had anything to eat today?" She picked up the appetizer menu in the middle of the table.

"I can't remember." His arm flung out and he grabbed it with his other hand.

Ignoring the unusual motions, she said, "The quesadilla is a good choice if you'd like an appetizer." She thought maybe some food in him would help to level him out.

"That sounds good." Rudy said, his gaze on the table.

"Would you order a chicken quesadilla and snag two glasses of water for us, please?" Dela asked Ross.

He nodded and walked over to the bar.

"What brings you here, Rudy?" she asked the man across the table from her.

"I came for the summit."

She sat up straighter and studied him. He was a person she wouldn't have forgotten. They hadn't questioned him. "Really? I thought most of the attendees had gone home."

"I can't. My car was stolen and the Indian police said I should call my insurance." He glanced up at her. "I don't have any insurance and no one to call to come get me."

"Why were you at the summit?" she asked as Ross brought over the glasses of water.

Rudy glanced around the room, his head jerking this way and that as he studied everyone in the place. "I get paid to do things."

"What kind of things? For who?" Dela was wondering if she'd found their killer.

"I leave notes, keep tabs on people, that sort of thing." He drank half the glass of water.

"Do you do that for the power company or the Save Our Fish group?"

He laughed, and said, "Save Our Fish don't have any money. And I don't do nothing for the rich. I help out the people. That's what Connie and I do."

Double frickin' shit! She'd been right about the woman. Ms. Oswood had conned this man into thinking he was helping the people. "What were you doing Wednesday night about two a.m.?"

"Wednesday night?" The man studied her, his eyes

bouncing. "How many days ago was that?"

"Four." Dela texted Quinn and Heath to get over to the casino. "The day all the Save Our Fish people arrived."

He nodded. "That afternoon, I checked into my room and Connie visited me. She asked me to slip some notes under some doors and to keep an eye on Mrs. Silva." He smiled. "I liked following her. She's pretty." His grin grew sappy. "And she's nice."

"She is nice. What did she say to you?" Dela asked.

"Nothing. I was sitting a couple of slot machines over from her and when she won on her machine, she looked around, smiled at me, and handed me the slip from her machine. "She'd won three hundred dollars." The awe in his voice made her wonder how he'd spent the money.

"How many notes did you deliver for Connie?" Her phone buzzed. A glance at the screen revealed it was Quinn saying he was on his way. Nothing yet from Heath.

"About a dozen." He sipped the water as Ross returned with the food. Rudy pulled the plate toward him and began eating.

"Did you read the notes?" Dela asked.

He shook his head. "Better I don't know. That's what Connie says."

"You never once peeked?" Dela urged.

"No. I did wait and watch someone read one. He looked angry." He put the triangle of tortilla and cheese down and shivered.

"Who was it? Do you know the person's name?" This was their best leverage against Connie. Rudy had to prove helpful and truthful.

"The big Indian man. He's been at all the summits. When I saw him open the door and look around, I knew he wasn't going to like the message. As soon as he read it and his face got angry, I hurried out of there."

"Tommy Darkhorse?" Dela asked, wondering why the man hadn't told them about the note slipped under his door.

Chapter Seventeen

Dela and Ross escorted Rudy across the casino floor toward the security office. Quinn walked through the casino entrance followed by Heath.

Dela hung back, knowing Ross would put the now lethargic man into the interview room.

Quinn wasn't dressed in his suit. He had on a long-sleeved flannel shirt, open in the front over a dark t-shirt, jeans, and athletic shoes. She preferred this look over his suits. Heath was also out of uniform, dressed in his usual jeans and t-shirt. Which would help when they talked with Rudy. Uniforms seemed to make him nervous.

"Why did you tell me to get over here? Do you have car trouble?" Quinn asked, stopping close to her.

Dela backed up as Heath stopped beside the FBI agent.

"No car trouble. Thank you both for coming." She smiled at Heath. "I have someone who says Connie

Oswood was paying him to intimidate people who wanted the dams breached."

Quinn put his hand out to open the door.

She placed a hand on his arm, stopping him. "You have to go easy with him. He's coming down off of something." Dela went on to tell the two how she'd come upon the man.

"You're taking the word of someone who is high?" Quinn crossed his arms and stared at her.

"Do you really think someone who was high would make something like that up? I mean, really. I would be skeptical if he'd said he was asked by a unicorn to poof glitter under the doors."

Heath laughed.

And she continued. "But he was specific. Right down to putting a message under Tommy Darkhorse's door. Who, by the way, didn't tell us about the threats he'd reccived."

Quinn continued to study her. "You think a woman who sends someone else to deliver threats would use her bare hands to kill someone?"

"No. She would send someone else to do it." Dela crossed her arms and glared at Quinn. Why couldn't he see that Connie Oswood was corrupt enough to have someone killed?

"Let's go check out his mental stability," Heath said, defusing the standoff.

The security office door opened. Margie stuck her head out. "Ross wants to know if you are coming in to ask the guy more questions?"

Dela pushed by Quinn and headed to the interview room. "Rudy, I have two friends who'd like to ask you some questions." Dela sat down at the table across from the tweaking man.

Quinn took the seat on her left and Heath placed a chair on her right and sat down.

"Who's he?" Rudy asked, giving Quinn a steady stare. Well, as steady as he could considering his head kept twitching. It appeared Quinn's short-cropped hair and stern demeanor bothered Rudy, but Heath's long hair and nonchalant attitude didn't bother him.

"I'm Quinn. Dela tells us you've been running errands for Connie Oswood. Can you tell me about them?"

Ross leaned down and asked Dela if he could get back to the floor. She nodded.

Once Ross left the room, Quinn asked his question again.

"Is he going to get me some more water?" Rudy asked. "I'm really thirsty."

Dela started to stand, but Heath put a hand on her arm. He stood, walked to the door, and disappeared.

"What can you tell me about Wednesday night?" Quinn asked.

"That's the night you asked me about?" Rudy asked Dela.

"Yes."

"I was hanging out at the slot machines, watching people. Mr. Silva and his wife got into a fight. Later I saw her get into an older car and leave." Rudy circled the tip of his index finger on the tabletop. He watched his finger go around and around. "While I was enjoying my reward for slipping notes under doors, I saw spiderman walking around on the building."

Dela glanced at Quinn who peered back at her.

"Spiderman?" they said in unison.

"Yeah. I was out sitting on the step of a semi behind the casino. I looked up at the building and Spiderman was climbing up the wall." He grinned. "I couldn't believe he was here. I called out to him, but I guess he didn't hear me."

"Do you remember what time that was?" Quinn asked.

"Nope. When he disappeared into a room, I went in and crashed in my room. I didn't look at the clock." Rudy jumped as the door opened.

Heath carried in a glass. He placed the water in front of Rudy, and asked, "What did I miss?"

"Rudy says Spiderman was on the side of the building Wednesday night." Dela offered. She wondered if there had been a man scaling the building to get to Silva's room.

Heath raised an eyebrow and sat down.

"What room are you staying in?" Quinn asked.

"None. I checked out this morning and my car had been stolen. When I asked Connie for help, she told me I was on my own. I found some stuff she gave me for helping her and decided I might as well get high since I couldn't do nothing else." Rudy grinned and then guzzled the water. "Augh! Brain freeze!" He gripped his head and wailed.

Quinn shot to his feet.

Dela glanced at Heath. "Do you have an idea where he can stay until he can get a car?"

Heath stood. "Yeah. I have someplace you can stay until you straighten out and get things figured out." He smiled at Quinn. "That is if you are through talking with him?"

Rudy stopped wailing and nodded, shoving the

glass of ice water to the middle of the table.

"Yeah. For now. Where are you taking him?"

Heath shrugged. "I'll see if Grandfather Thunder will let Rudy stay in his trailer. He has it for the same situation for tribal members."

"Not Sherry and Trey's trailer," Dela said, worried that the single mother and her son would have to put up with this tweaker. She'd gone through enough having been kidnapped by human traffickers less than six months earlier.

"No. He has a small camp trailer. They will be fine. I put new locks on her door and fixed all the things Grandfather had been promising but didn't have the energy to do."

"I bet he's happy you are back," she said.

"Yeah. I'd rather hang out and do things for him than be at my mom's house. I hope to be out of there soon." He winked at her and stood, motioning for Rudy to get to his feet as well. "I'll let you both know if I learn anything new."

Dela nodded and the two left the room. She wished she had a way to get rid of Quinn.

"What do you plan to do with the information you heard?" Quinn asked.

"I plan on watching footage from the floors below ten and see who went into the rooms directly below ten-twenty. It had to have been the killer that Rudy saw scaling the building." Dela backed up so she didn't have to crane her neck to peer into Quinn's eyes.

"That's all you're going to do? You weren't planning on heading to Idaho to contact Connie Oswood?"

"No. I do plan on calling Tommy Darkhorse to ask

him what the note said that Rudy slipped under his door." She smiled. "I'll leave Ms. Oswood up to you. After all, you have federal jurisdiction. I'm only interested in what happened at this casino."

He studied her for a few seconds, before giving a slight nod and walking toward the door.

"Hey? What did you learn from Dan Germaine?" she asked.

"He's on a six-week vacation in Europe and I haven't been able to catch up to him." He shrugged and walked out of the interview room.

She let out a deep breath and spun out of the room to find Margie watching Quinn's back as it disappeared out of the security office. Dela shook her head. "Don't you have something better to do than watch Special Agent Pierce?"

"Not when he wears those tight jeans," Margie said and answered the ringing phone.

Dela shook her head and walked out of the security office and over to the keylock to enter the surveillance room. She tapped her security card on the box and the wall moved, allowing her entrance.

The four surveillance members glanced at the door as she entered.

"Is Marty back there today?" she asked.

"No, it's Farley," Marie said, returning her gaze to her screens.

Dela hadn't dealt with Marty's trainee. She opened the door to Marty's domain and found a young man, she judged to be in his twenties, with long hair, a big baggy t-shirt with a rock band insignia, jogging pants, and moccasins.

He swung the chair around at her entrance. "You're

Dela, the head of security."

"Yes, I am." He reminded her of Travis, the young man remodeling her house. "You must be Farley."

He grinned showing off dazzling white teeth. "I am. Marty said to help you however you needed it."

She walked over and took her usual chair, propping her prosthesis on the box under the table. "I need you to pull up the video on floors nine and eight in the hallway for rooms nine-twenty and eight-twenty."

"Do you have a time frame and date?" He started tapping the keyboard.

"Wednesday night, starting at midnight." She leaned back in her chair and waited for the feed to appear on the monitor in front of her.

♠ ♣ ♥ ♦

Two hours later and only confirming the people who went into the rooms directly below 1020 were the actual occupants, Dela leaned back in her chair. What was she missing? Was there really a person scaling the outside wall of the building?

She snapped her fingers. "Do we have surveillance cameras on the roof?"

"Sorry. No. There's no need. Only employees are allowed on the roof."

"Which means they would have to use the employee elevator. Can you pull that up for Wednesday night, starting at midnight?" She leaned forward, expecting to see someone she didn't know getting on the elevator.

They fast-forwarded to each person who used the elevator on the first floor, stopping to determine if they were an employee. They all checked out.

"This is going to be time-consuming, but I need

you to follow each of them up and see if any of them went to the roof." She sat up. "I'm going to check on things and head home." She wrote her cell number on a slip of paper. "Call me if you find someone going up to the roof."

"You want me to call even if it's like three in the morning?" Farley asked.

"No. You can leave a note for me here. But if you discover it before ten tonight, call."

She walked out of the room and the surveillance area. Standing out on the casino floor, she scanned the area for her guards. The flute music was audible over the faint machine noises. Even the smoke scent was stale and less forceful. She rarely spent a Sunday afternoon or evening in the casino now that she was head of security. It was the complete opposite of a Friday or Saturday evening.

In the security office, she walked over to her desk. "Margie, I'm going home. If something comes up, give me a call. Otherwise, you can leave Kenny a message I'll be in at ten tomorrow morning."

"Got it. You going to do anything fun?" The woman studied her with a wide grin on her face.

"I'm going to eat ice cream and watch a movie with my dog." Her answer wiped the grin off Margie's face. The woman had expected her to say she was meeting up with the FBI agent. That wasn't happening. While her body may heat thinking about him, she preferred the easy camaraderie she had with Heath. Her high school boyfriend was less complicated than the FBI Special Agent.

Walking out the back of the casino to her car, Dela stopped and faced the building. Looking up, she studied the side of the casino and the roof. Before she left, she wanted to take a look at the roof. From the structures she could see, it would be easy enough to tie off a rope and rappel down the side of the building.

Walking back into the building, she waved away Margie's question and walked out into the hallway connecting all the behind-the-scenes departments of the casino. She walked over to the service elevator, hit the button, and waited. Banging came from the maintenance room. And the hum of the large washers and dryers in the laundry room echoed down the halls on the antiscptic scent of the detergent.

The doors swished open. This elevator was twice the size of the elevators that lifted guests to their floors. She hit the door close button and then the button marked roof. Starting at the bottom floor, no security access was needed. However, if someone had accessed the service elevator on any of the other floors, they would need a security badge.

The elevator ground its way up to the roof. The doors opened and a burst of wind slapped Dela in the face, taking her breath away. She gasped and faced the other direction to suck in air. Once she had her bearings figured out, she walked to the backside of the building, studying every nook and cranny for anything that might have been left behind or inadvertently lost by whoever scaled the casino.

The mid-thigh height of the wall would have been easy enough to slip over. She looked out at where her car was parked and over to the left where the RVs and semis parked. If she believed Rudy, he had been over there. Which meant room 1020 was on that side of the building. Dela walked over to the northeast, again, scanning the building for any sign of climbing gear.

Her phone buzzed. Her mom.

"Hi mom," she answered.

"Are you home? I made you some brownies. I thought I'd come see how the remodel was going." Her mom came over once a week to see the progress on the house.

"I'm not home at the moment. But I should be there by six if you want to stay for dinner." Even as she invited her mom, she knew there was nothing in her kitchen that would make a dinner that wouldn't have her mom bringing over meals every day.

"I have a casserole I was going to take to Grandfather Thunder. How about I bring him along and we can all enjoy it and the brownies?" she asked.

While her home wasn't ready for visitors, she knew the only right answer was to agree. "Sure. But bring a couple of folding chairs. I still don't have furniture for company."

"Wonderful. I'll let Grandfather Thunder know. See you at six."

The phone went silent. Dela glanced at the time on the device. She had an hour to finish exploring and get home.

She noticed a mark on the edge of the cement wall. It appeared as if something, like a rope, had rubbed back and forth, sawing a mark on the edge. She took a photo with her phone. Glancing around, she noticed a cylinder-shaped hunk of concrete sticking up from the rooftop. The shape was about three feet high and hollow. She stared into the cylinder. Something was coiled up at the bottom. She set her camera on flash and held it down in the hole, taking a picture. When she looked at the photo she'd taken, it showed a coiled-up rock climbing rope.

How convenient that a climbing rope was here on the roof. Or had the person brought it with them and then left it behind so they wouldn't be seen carrying it? Which was stupid, considering after seeing the footage and knowing no one had gone into the victim's room, they would start looking for other ways the killer entered the room.

She sent the two photos to Heath. *This is what I found on the roof. Rudy did see Spiderman, sort of.*

I'll be right there. Heath texted back.

I can't hang around. I have to meet Mom and Grandfather Thunder at my place for dinner.

I know. I've been invited too. He added a smiley face to the text. *See you in 10.*

"Frickin' shit!" Dela shouted. All she needed was her mom and Grandfather Thunder trying to matchmake her and Heath.

She might as well sit tight and watch the mountains someplace out of the wind. Sliding down to sit with her back against the hollow pillar, she studied the Blue Mountains and thought about her hike that morning with Mugshot.

Chapter Eighteen

Heath arrived on the roof with a tribal officer. While the officer took photos of the mark on the wall, Heath helped Dela to her feet. "I figured you'd be digging up dirt on Ms. Oswood, not hanging out on a rooftop."

Dela released his hands and pointed into the concrete tube. "You'll find a climbing rope in there." She walked a few steps away. "I let Quinn deal with her. I can't hold my anger when I'm around that woman. Best to let someone who understands that type talk to her." She hoped the resentment she felt toward the woman didn't come through in her voice.

"Yeah, you've never been the kid gloves type of person," Heath said for her only and then raised his voice. "Bailey, take photos of the rope in here and bag it. Then I want photos of this whole rooftop and anything you find bagged."

"Yes, sir," the younger officer said.

"When you get done, take it all to the station. I'm off duty but will look it all over in the morning." Heath waved for Dela to walk toward the elevator door.

She started walking, and he fell into step beside her. "I never thought you'd be someone in charge, but you handle yourself well."

He chuckled. "Yeah, while I didn't care to be bossed around, I found you get more work done if you do give orders."

They pushed the button for the elevator.

"What made you think to come up here?" Heath asked as the doors opened.

Dela stepped in and told him how she'd watched the video footage and no one other than the occupants had entered any of the rooms above or below 1020. Which led her to believe the killer had climbed down from the roof.

"You always did have a mind for problem-solving." They stepped out of the service elevator and walked down the hall and through the security office.

Margie's eyebrows rose seeing her with Heath.

"Now, I'm leaving," she said to the security guard. She opened the back door, allowing Heath to exit ahead of her. She made sure the door locked and pointed to her car. "Since it's a quarter to six, you might as well follow me home."

"See you there." Heath strode over to his pickup.

Dela slid into her car and headed home. She was eager to see Mugshot and was excited to show off the mural in her bedroom to her mom, but she wasn't looking forward to any leading questions from her mother or Grandfather Thunder about her and Heath.

♠ ♣ ♥ ♦

When Dela arrived at her house, Mom and Grandfather Thunder were in the backyard with Mugshot. While her mom had been against her getting such a large dog, the animal had warmed her mother up to him. Grandfather Thunder and her mom sat in folding chairs, they must have brought with them, and were taking turns throwing a ball for Mugshot to retrieve. Dela and the big dog had started this activity when he needed exercise but not too much. Now they jogged around the neighborhood.

Before letting the two know she was home, she tidied up the place, even though she was pretty sure her mom had probably looked through all the windows she could before sitting down to play ball.

Opening the French door onto the small patio, Dela stepped out. "I see you two made yourselves at home."

Her mom jumped, but Grandfather Thunder just turned a sly smile her direction. Mugshot forgot his ball and ran over to gently place the top of his head against her thigh so she could scratch his ears. Their usual ritual when she came home.

She rubbed his wide ears and scratched around the base of them. "Heath should—"

"Here," Heath said from behind her.

"While you help Grandfather Thunder get his chair in the house, Heath can help me get the food out of my car." Mom jumped up and hurried into the house, heading straight for the front door.

Dela gave the eighty-something-year-old man an arm to use to raise up out of the chair.

"Your mom is bossier when she's around you," he said.

Dela laughed. "Yeah, I seem to bring that out in

189

people."

Grandfather Thunder laughed, and said, "I don't think so. Anyone who knows you for more than five minutes knows you are capable of taking care of yourself." He pointed west. "And others."

It took her several seconds to realize what he meant. She touched the healing bruises on her face.

"I couldn't let that man kill his wife." She carried both chairs into the dining room and set them at the card table, wishing her house was finished.

"You are a true warrior." The man sat back down in his chair.

The door banged open, and Heath walked in carrying a large cardboard box.

"Mom, I thought it was a casserole and brownies," Dela said as her mom followed carrying another smaller box and a thermos.

"That box has the casserole, French bread, salad, and the brownies. This box has a set of dishes that made me think of you, so I bought them at the second-hand store."

Dela had three utility-style plates and two mugs she'd bought that were used as bowls for cereal and ice cream. She opened the box her mom sat on the card table. "Mom, these are perfect!"

"There were only three large plates, but I'll see if I can find some online to get you more," Mom said as Dela picked up a cereal bowl. The dark brown bowl had a band on the top two-thirds that looked like white birch limbs with tan leaves. The set reminded her of the mountains. The plates had a two-inch band of the same design around their edges and the mugs were similar to the bowls.

Dela hugged her mom as Heath grabbed the box and started rinsing the dishes.

"We might as well use these to eat off of tonight," he said.

"Let me do that," Dela said, moving Heath away from the sink. "You'll need to find something to use as a chair to sit at the table with us."

He surrendered the sink and left through the front door. A minute later, as Dela dried and set the plates on the table, he returned with a folding chair.

"Where did you get that?" she asked.

"I put it in my pickup after I was here the other night." Heath grinned and set it at the side of the table without a chair.

She ignored the way it felt as if the air had been sucked out of the room at his mention of having visited her before.

Mom had the food on the table and was pouring iced tea from the thermos into the coffee mugs.

"You know, I have iced tea, Mom," Dela said.

"I wasn't sure. You didn't want us to all go thirsty." Her mom smiled at everyone seated at the table.

"I have water. It comes out of the faucet." Dela didn't like how her mom was making her feel inferior.

"This is good," Grandfather Thunder said, taking over the conversation. He, Heath, and Mom talked about some of the Thunder family members who still lived on the reservation.

Dela let her mind wander to the discoveries she'd made today. Uppermost in her thoughts was trying to figure out if it wasn't an employee who used the service elevator to get to the rooftop, then who did? And had they brought the rope with them? Or if it was there, how had they known it would be there?

"Dela?" A hand waved in front of her face, just grazing her nose.

She flung her head back as if it had been a fist catching her off guard.

Heath held both hands up. "Your mom asked you a question."

Swiveling her head in the opposite direction, she encountered her mom's worried expression. "What?"

"I asked when you were going to be ready for flooring." Mom studied her.

"Sorry. I was problem-solving." She glanced at Heath. He nodded he knew what she was talking about. "Travis finished up in here this week. I plan to go see what I can find next week when I have time."

Her mom sat up straighter. "If you tell me what you're looking for, I can pick up samples for you to look at here in the house. That would give you a better idea of what they will look like."

Dela liked the idea of not having to run around looking at different flooring. "I was thinking about the easy-to-install plank flooring. I'm sure Travis and his crew could put it down for me. The sooner I can get it in, the sooner I can get furniture and a bed."

"You need to see the mural Toby painted on her bedroom wall," Heath said.

Her mom's neck popped when her head twisted fast in Heath's direction. "You've been in my daughter's bedroom?"

"It's not like he didn't spend time in it when we were in high school," Dela joked.

Which put her on the receiving end of one of her

mother's famous scowls.

"Toby is slow but very talented," Grandfather Thunder said, pushing up from the chair. "I would like to see this."

Dela scooted her chair back and led the group down the hall to her bedroom. The minute she stepped into the room she realized this was a mistake. Her makeshift bed of blankets on the floor would mortify her mom. Waving her arms, to keep her mom's vision in the air, on the walls, she said, "This is a beautiful abstract of the Blue Mountains and this will definitely catch all my bad dreams."

"Nice." Grandfather Thunder said.

Her mom oooed before her gaze landed on the blankets. "You're sleeping on the hard floor? I thought you had an air mattress. The one you used when you'd go camping."

"It was old. The first night it wouldn't hold air so I threw it away."

Heath's phone rang. He stepped out into the hall.

Before Dela could field another question from her mom, he stepped back in.

"I have to go. Grandfather's guest is on the move." He peered into Dela's eyes. "I'll take a rain check on the brownies."

She nodded and he left. Without looking at either her mom or Grandfather Thunder, Dela led them over to the exercise room and extra bedroom.

"I guess you'll be making this room into an office?" her mom asked, as they stood inside the extra bedroom.

Dela weighed whether or not to tell her mom Heath would be her roommate and he'd occupy this room. She opted to wait until he was moved in since he wasn't here to field her questions. "Yes. it will be my office. Let's go have dessert."

♠ ♣ ♥ ♦

Dela had cleaned up after her company left and had just settled into her chair after a shower, when someone knocked on the door. Mugshot growled low in his throat. Dela shoved out of the chair and onto her crutches making as little noise as she could. Though she could have made as much as she wanted now that Mugshot was barking.

She stood to the side of the door, clutching a baseball bat in her hand. She kept the piece of athletic equipment by her chair. "Who is it?"

"I'm back for my raincheck on dessert," Heath said.

She opened the door and found a twin-size mattress. Backing up she allowed him access. "What is that for? You aren't moving in until the house is finished." She sat on the arm of the recliner as he walked in and lay the mattress on its side.

"It's for you until you get a bed." He took off down the hallway to her room with the mattress.

"I would like to say, take it back, but after trying to sleep on the hard floor last night, I'm happy you thought of this." She stopped at the doorway. "It's not yours, is it? You aren't sleeping on the floor because of this."

"Grandfather Thunder called me when he arrived home and told me to swing by when I was finished and take this to you." Heath studied her. "He is your knight in shining armor, not me."

She ignored his curiosity about if she thought he

was a knight. "What happened with Rudy?"

"Turned out he thought he could walk to the casino and get a drink. I picked him up on my way to Grandfather Thunder's. I took him to Mission Market and bought him some beer and chips and bread so he could make toast in the morning. I suggested he'd be safer staying put for a few days until his car was found. That way we could get it to him easier. He gave me the make, model, and license so I could put a bulletin out about it."

"Didn't someone already do that when he reported it missing?" Dela led the way back to the kitchen and the remaining brownies her mom had left for her.

"They took down the information but didn't do anything else. I added it was possible it had something to do with the murder and that gave the hunt for it more credibility." Heath sat in the folding chair he'd brought in earlier. "Do you have any milk to go with this?"

"Yeah." She grabbed the jug of milk out of the fridge. "Did the officer you left on the roof find anything else?"

"No. Anyway, not that he could see. I'll go over the photos tomorrow and get the items we did find to a forensic lab." He picked up a brownie and studied her. "Did you tell any of this to Quinn?"

Her face heated. He was part of the investigation, but she hadn't wanted to call and have him think she didn't trust him with Connie Oswood. "No. He took off to question Connie Oswood about her involvement with Rudy and the threats to the summit attendees. I figure he'll get caught up tomorrow when he gets back."

"What is it between you two?" Heath bit his brownie and chewed watching her. "Other than the incident in Iraq."

Dela wasn't sure why FBI Special Agent Quinn Pierce irritated her so much. "Maybe because he is so condescending. Or it could be how he treats me as if I can't take care of myself. Or my favorite, he thinks he has some power over me, not just because he is FBI but because he's male and I'm female."

Heath started laughing. "If I was the jealous type, I'd be worried you were falling for him."

Dela snorted and spit the bite she'd just taken out onto the napkin. "Falling for him? Now you're starting to sound like the women at the casino. I can guarantee you that I am not falling for him. I'm uncomfortable around him. I don't feel like I can be myself."

"Like you can with me. I have been likened to a faithful old dog." He said the last sentence with the most animosity she'd ever seen or heard from him.

"No! I would never call you a faithful old dog. Who did that?" She handed him another brownie.

"A woman I had dated for three years and when I asked her to marry me, she said she didn't need a faithful old dog, she needed a man who made her blood boil and her body ache for him." Heath smashed the brownie under his fist. Not with a loud thump, just slow even pressure.

"She wasn't the right one for you then." Dela studied her friend's face. Her heart did quicken when she watched him and anticipated his visits. She slid her hand across the table, touching his fist. "Fate has a way of bringing the right people together at the right time."

His gaze raised to hers. "Like now?"

"Could be."

Mugshot walked to the door and whined.

She released Heath's hand and he stood, letting the dog out.

"Want me to help you make your bed before I leave?" Heath stood beside her chair, gazing down at her.

"I'll be fine. Go on home and thank Grandfather Thunder for the mattress. When I get the flooring in, I could use your help and pickup to get furniture."

"I thought you asked Travis and his gang to help." Heath studied her.

"I'd rather bring it home a piece or two at a time and not be overwhelmed with having to place it all at once." With as haphazard as her free time was, the thought of having a pile of furniture in her living room made her nauseous.

"It's a deal. Talk to you tomorrow if I learn anything new." He leaned down and kissed the top of her head.

Her body warmed. It had been a long time since she'd had any affection from anyone other than her mother. "Thanks. I'll do the same."

He walked to the front door and let himself out.

Dela waited until Mugshot came back in before they headed to the bedroom and she flopped a sheet over the mattress and topped it off with the blankets. She crawled in and Mugshot lay his head on the bed next to hers.

She wondered if Quinn had learned anything from Connie.

Chapter Nineteen

The following morning her phone rang as she walked through the casino parking lot to the back of the building.

"Hello?"

"It's Quinn. Where are you?"

"Just coming in the employee entrance. Where are you?"

"Pulling off the interstate. I'll meet you in the coffee shop."

"Do we need to include Heath in this conversation? He and I discovered someone had a rope up on the roof and may have rappelled down to the victim's room."

He cussed and then said, "I guess so. You call him, and I'll meet you in five in the coffee shop."

The line went silent. She grinned wondering if he was mad she wanted Heath included or because they had found some evidence while he was off chasing Connie.

"Morning boss," Oliver, an older Umatilla man, said when she entered the building. He had been put on the job of watching the employees going in and out of the building because he had been caught falling asleep out on the floor. And if he didn't have a job, he'd be out on the street.

"Morning, Oliver. Tell Kenny to meet me in the coffee shop when he gets in." She dropped her purse on her desk and headed out onto the casino floor. She crossed through the slot machines. Monday mornings were always quiet. It was the best time to work on schedules and discuss security issues for upcoming events.

She called Heath, stopping in the middle of the machines.

"Hey, I was about to call you. I just finished looking over all the photos Bailey took last evening."

"Good. Quinn has requested our presence at the coffee shop here at the casino. Can you make it?" She spotted the FBI agent striding from the entrance toward the coffee shop. "He just arrived."

"I'll be there in ten."

She hung up, scanned the casino floor, and walked to the coffee shop. At the door, Dela inhaled the scent of cinnamon as she spotted Quinn taking a seat in the booth farthest from the door that faced the entrance.

The waitress intercepted her on her way across the room. "What would you like?"

"Coffee." Dela continued and took the seat across the table from Quinn. "How did your trip to see Ms. Oswood go?"

He scowled. "I'd rather not say until Seaver arrives. Any idea when he'll get here?"

"When I called, he said it would be ten minutes."

Quinn grunted and nodded.

The waitress arrived with the coffees.

"There will be one more person joining us. Could you bring out another cup and a carafe of coffee?" Dela asked.

The woman nodded.

Dela stopped her before she'd moved away. "And how about three cinnamon rolls?"

The waitress's face lit up. "We have fresh ones this morning."

"I know. The aroma is making my mouth water."

As the waitress hurried away, Quinn ran a hand over his freshly shaved face.

"Did you stay in Idaho last night?" she asked, wondering at how his visit had gone.

"Yeah, by the time I arrived at Ms. Oswood's residence, talked with her, and wrote up a report, I was tired. I got a room there and left early this morning."

Heath strode toward the booth at the same time the waitress arrived with the carafe, cup, and cinnamon rolls.

Dela stood, allowing him to slide to the inside of the booth while she remained on the outside edge. "Thank you," she said to the waitress.

"I'm starved, thank you whoever thought of the cinnamon rolls." Heath grabbed one and started eating.

"Why don't you start off with what you learned yesterday evening," Dela said to Quinn, allowing Heath time to fill his stomach before relaying what he'd learned.

"As you can imagine, Ms. Oswood denied knowing anything about Rudy. I have agents looking into her phone records to see if she contacted him that way."

Dela shook her head at the same time Heath said, "She didn't. According to Rudy she would meet up with him at his room at the summits and give him his instructions." He turned slightly on the bench to look at Dela. "He said he was in one-thirty-nine on the first floor and she paid for his room. You can check on who paid the bill and have surveillance watch his room to see if she did visit him."

She nodded, pulling out her phone and making a note of the room number.

"Did you get her to tell you anything helpful?" Dela asked.

"An agent who was watching her since her arrival back in Boise said she drove out to the victim's home yesterday. She was well-received by Mrs. Silva, but when the woman left, a man, fitting the description of Ben Gibbons, stopped her as she was driving away and it looked like they had a heated argument. When I asked Ms. Oswood about it, she just said, he thought she was someone Mr. Silva had been fooling around with and thought it was in poor taste that she'd visited the man's wife."

"Why would Ben think the victim had been fooling around with Connie unless he'd been following Mr. Silva?" She wondered what Ben did for a living. "What do we know about Ben?"

Heath pulled out his logbook and flipped through the pages. "He was working construction up until last year. Then worked for a bit at Yellowhawk in maintenance. Until he was fired for stealing drugs."

"And now he's become his rich cousin's shoulder to cry on." Dela didn't like the idea of Stacy Silva being hurt again. While she and the woman had nothing in common, she had felt a connection with her when they'd talked. "Do you think it's a coincidence that he was here to pick up the pieces for Stacy?"

Quinn narrowed his eyes, studying her. "You think Ben killed Silva and then ingratiated himself into Stacy's life?"

She shrugged. "It's a theory. What do you think?" She leveled her gaze on Heath.

"I don't think the timeline works. If he drove Mrs. Silva to the Rose's on Wildhorse Mountain, leaving here at one, he wouldn't have been back here until three in the morning. Do you really think Rudy sat out in the parking lot for two hours?" Heath picked up his cup of coffee.

"No. I like Ben for this. Of the suspects we have, who else could have scaled the building and entered through the balcony?" Dela had another thought. "Have any of the fingerprints come back from the balcony railing?"

"I'm sure from lack of fingerprints in the whole room that whoever strangled our victim was wearing gloves," Quinn stated.

It was Dela's turn to scowl. "What about the hairs that were found?"

"They have the hairs classified as two male and one female—the dark brown ones and the bleached blonde is female. We know where that one came from. I'm having someone go over the photos of the wife's clothing in the closet to see if it might have been from a garment." Quinn pulled out his phone and slid his finger across the screen, scrolling.

"Wait, you said two male?" Dela's adrenalin

started pumping, feeling like this was a clue. "We know about Tommy Darkhorse being in the room. One of those is his. But if there was another male in that room with long dark hair, it has to be the killer."

"That makes sense," Heath said, perking up.

"They have the DNA samples. We just need to find a match." Quinn glanced up from his phone. "What do you have in mind?"

"I'm going to pay Butch and Melba a visit. Maybe say that Stacy left something and asked that I bring it to her. That will get me into the bedrooms and I can find something with Ben's DNA on it to use as a comparison. If we discover it was him, then we can work on the evidence to convict him."

"It can't hurt," Heath said.

"You aren't going there alone," Quinn said.

She glared at the FBI agent. "The only people there are Butch and Melba. You said Ben was still in Idaho. And it would look suspicious if you go with me." Dela stood at the sight of Kenny walking into the coffee shop. "I have casino business to deal with. I'll drive out there after lunch. Is there anything else either of you want to add?" Her gaze flicked over the two men.

"Yes. The photos from the roof don't prove who climbed down, but we do know someone did use the rope found in the turret to climb down the side of the building. The mark on the ledge is a perfect fit for the rope and there is a worn spot where it would have hung over the edge." Heath shoved a file across the table to Quinn. "Everything found on the roof has been sent to the forensic lab. We just need to figure out how he got up there and we should find him."

Dela nodded. "Let me know what you both find

out. I have my casino job to do." She picked up her half-eaten cinnamon roll and coffee, made eye contact with Kenny, and nodded her head toward a different booth.

They met at the booth and began discussing casino business. When she'd finished her roll and coffee, they moved to the security office. Heath and Quinn were still sitting in the coffee shop.

Quinn walked into the security office an hour later. "Got a minute?"

She was finishing up schedules for the following week. "Yes."

"There's no need for you to go to the Rose house. I asked if the DNA from the three dark hairs had shown any familial characteristics. The lab tech said no. That means it can't be Ben if he and Stacy are related."

Dela studied him. "Is this your way of keeping me from going to Wildhorse Mountain?"

He ran a hand over his chin and mouth as if holding in what he wanted to say. He dropped his hand and said, "There is no reason for you to go up there and try to get a sample. The science says the hairs aren't connected. And even Heath said there was no way Ben could have made it back down here quick enough."

"Okay. I won't go looking for a DNA sample. I have a phone call to make." She stared at him and then the door.

Quinn studied her. "I'm going to see if I can dig up anything else on Ms. Oswood and Mr. Wallen."

"That sounds like good suspects to check out." This time she waved her hand, motioning for him to leave.

He strode to the door, opened it, and glanced back,

before walking through.

"The man is too uptight," Oliver said.

"Yes, he is." Dela agreed and dug through the sticky notes on her desk for the number of Tommy Darkhorse. She found the slip of paper and dialed the number.

"Hello?" Tommy answered.

"Mr. Darkhorse, this is Dela Alvaro with the Spotted Pony Casino security. I have a couple of questions about the night Mr. Silva was murdered."

"I told the tribal police and the FBI everything I know."

"Well, that's where I think you're wrong. I learned yesterday that you received a note under your hotel door that made you mad. Care to share what the note said?" She had a pen poised over her sticky pad.

"How did you hear about that?" His tone was low and menacing.

"From the person who delivered it." She wasn't going to mention Rudy. But she did wonder if Tommy knew him since Rudy said he'd been at other summits.

"I can tell you, I'm pretty sure it came from the power company that Kevin worked for. The message said, 'Either vote against the breaching or find more than the fish dead.'"

"What do you think that meant?" Dela had a suspicion nothing would have happened. It would have been hard to threaten that many people with bodily harm and then follow through with it. It would draw too much attention.

"It was obvious someone planned to harm people. I tried to see who left the note and asked others if they had received any. They wouldn't say. But I could tell they were scared to admit it." Tommy's tone had become more conversational and less menacing.

"Was the note handwritten or typed? Do you still have it?" Dela wondered if there would be prints on the paper.

"Typed. I crumpled it up and tossed it in the wastebasket."

"Why didn't you bring it up when you were questioned? It could have been taken in as evidence." Why hadn't this man been more cooperative? Was he worried he would be caught up in the murder?

"I-I couldn't believe Kevin was dead and that it had been murder. Then I wondered if that was the first person to die and I would be next if I said anything." Fear didn't quiver the man's voice. While he didn't want to die, he didn't fear it.

"Like making a statement by knocking off the person who was trying to bring the sides together?" She wondered again if Silva had been killed because of the email he'd sent his boss. It had been pushing for what the power company didn't want. Would they have gone so far as to kill the messenger?

"I was told you are friends with Mrs. Silva's brother. What can you tell me about the family?" She hoped to learn more about Ben's connection with the family.

"Did Stacy tell you I was keeping an eye on Kevin for her? Though she had nothing to worry about. I told her Connie Oswood was sucking up to all the men at the summits trying to sway their allegiance." Tommy gave the impression he didn't care for Connie.

"Yes. That is who I heard it from. What do you know about the Rose family relatives?"

"Nice old couple. They were at a few of the family events I have attended with Joseph, Stacy's brother."

"Did you see their grandson, Ben, at any of these events? He would be about five or six years younger than Stacy." She didn't want to put ideas or words in his head. But she wanted to know more about him.

"I don't remember him. You could ask Stacy."

This was a hard one. She didn't want to get Stacy in the middle of this and get her hurt if Ben was the man who killed her husband. "Thanks. I'll do that. Can you think of anything else that happened the night Kevin died that might help us?"

"No, I wish I could. Kevin was one of the good guys."

"Thank you for answering my questions." Dela ended the call and remembered they needed the surveillance footage of Rudy's room to catch Connie in a lie.

Chapter Twenty

Sitting in the surveillance office with Farley, Dela's eyes felt like they were spinning in her head.

"Can you slow down the fast forward? It's giving me a headache." They had watched the tape over and over again and never saw Connie make contact with Rudy at his room. Was the man lying? Had he really worked for Connie or was he trying to get her in trouble?

Her phone buzzed. Without looking at the caller, she slid her finger across the front and answered. "Hello?"

"The little weasel left," Heath said, through what sounded like clenched teeth.

"What weasel?" The minute the words were out she knew.

"Rudy." They said at the same time.

"He wasn't arrested for anything," she said.

"No. But where did he go, and why, if his car was

stolen like he said." The clunk of his boot heels echoed through the phone. He was pacing somewhere with solid floors.

"He put more heat on Connie and told us about the person scaling the building. We have proof about the messages, I talked to Tommy Darkhorse today and he told me about the message he'd received."

Heath started to say something and she cut him off. "He didn't save it." She told him what the message had said.

"Rudy didn't lie about the messages." That seemed to ease Heath some.

"But I've been going over the surveillance video and not once during his stay at the hotel does Connie go near his room."

"Maybe he said that to keep you from looking where they did meet up. She spent a lot of time in the Pony Bar and Grill. Can you have someone go over that footage to find them talking or her handing him something?" Excitement trickled into Heath's voice.

"I'll have Farley look into it. In the meantime, are you with Grandfather Thunder?" The old man knew everything about everyone on the reservation.

"Yeah?"

"Ask him about the Rose family. Especially Ben. I just have a feeling this murder wasn't about the fish."

"I can do that. How about I come over tonight and help you finish off that casserole? I can fill you in on what I've learned."

She chuckled. "What and leave Quinn out?"

"You can invite him too, but I don't think there was that much casserole left over." She heard the smile in Heath's voice.

"I'll call him with an update before I head home. That way we won't be actually leaving him out of the loop. He'll just think our checking up on Ben isn't necessary anyway." Who did Quinn think killed Kevin Silva? He didn't think Connie had or Ben, who did that leave? The boss.

"See you then." Heath ended the call.

Dela tipped her head this way and that, releasing the tension in her neck.

"Having dinner with someone?" Farley asked.

"My personal life is that, personal. I would like you to do a follow of this woman." She pulled up the photo she had of Connie on her phone. "From the time she arrived at the casino to when she checked out. I want to see everyone she meets up with. And tally if she meets some of the people more than once."

"I didn't find any employees using the elevator to go to the roof," he said.

"That's the only way to get up there," she mused.

"Unless you use the fire stairs." Farley tapped away at the keyboard.

"Fire stairs… Why didn't I think of that?"

"Because why would anyone be on the roof if there was a fire?" he continued to type.

"Call me when you get that done." She stood, catching her balance when her left foot tingled from falling asleep.

"I'm sorry if I made you dizzy from fast-forwarding at warp speed," Farley apologized.

"It's ok." Better he thought she was dizzy than knowing her balance was compromised because she didn't have feeling in either foot.

She walked through the surveillance room and out

onto the casino floor. If she had all day to climb the flights of the three fire escapes she might have started at the bottom, but instead, she took the elevator to the top floor, then pushed open the fire exit door on the side closest to room 1020 and scanned the stairs leading upward. There was a layer of dust. Fire stairs were only maintained so that there wasn't anything hindering their use.

The dust showed footprints going both up and down the stairs. This was how the killer made it to the roof. Not by the service elevator. This was the easiest way for someone to not be seen. Rather than go up, she held onto the rail and hugged the wall to not compromise the prints and headed down, following the footprints she noted they came onto the staircase several floors down from the roof. She pushed the door open and found herself on the tenth floor. Had the person been someone staying on this floor or only used this floor because they were watching to see when the victim would be alone?

She texted Heath and Quinn. *The killer used the fire stairs from floor ten to the roof.*

I'll get someone over to take photos. Heath replied.

I'll send over Shaffer to take a look. Quinn replied.

Dela headed to the elevator, taking it to the casino floor. There she walked into the security office and called Farley. "When you get the video on Connie Oswood done, I would like all the video footage for the hall outside the fire exit door on floor ten from midnight until three in the morning. I'll check it out tomorrow."

"Right! Because you have a dinner date tonight." Farley reminded her of a creature from her childhood.

Barney the Purple Dinosaur. He was cute but irritating.

She ended the call and picked up her purse. "I'm going home. I'll see you tomorrow, Oliver."

"I'll be here," the old man answered, looking up from a game of solitaire he was playing.

It was early enough she and Mugshot could get in a run and a shower before Heath arrived for leftovers.

♠ ♣ ♥ ♦

The table was set with the dishes her mother had brought over the night before and the casserole was warming up in the oven when Dela walked over to the door and opened it.

Heath stood on the other side, holding a six-pack of her favorite beer and a quart of her favorite ice cream.

"You know how to spoil a person," she said, stepping back to allow him entrance.

"I just know what you like."

"I'm surprised you remember after all these years." She took the ice cream, shoving it in the freezer compartment of her fridge.

Heath put two bottles of beer on the table and placed the rest in the fridge. "The two years we dated were the best two years of my youth."

Her gaze collided with his. "Mine too. When I was deployed, I would think about some of the fun and stupid things we did in high school. It made things easier."

He unscrewed the tops of the beers and handed her one. Raising his in a toast he said, "Here's to good friends."

She clinked her bottle against his. "Good friends." Saying it and seeing his acknowledgment in his eyes made her feel almost normal.

"Want to swap news or eat?" she asked, taking a drink and putting the bottle down.

"We can swap while we eat. I'm hungry. All I had today was the cinnamon roll and some weird cookie Martha Pile gave Grandfather Thunder." Heath shuddered.

Dela laughed. "Grab the salad out of the fridge. I'll put the casserole on the table."

They sat, filled their plates, and had several bites before Dela started telling Heath what she'd learned from Tommy Darkhorse, the surveillance video, and the fire stairs.

"According to Grandfather Thunder, Ben has been in trouble since he started school. He's not a Rose biologically. He is the son of a woman who married into the Rose family after having Ben."

"Which means his DNA wouldn't match Stacy's." The knowledge boosted her confidence in following her gut.

Heath held up his fork with salad on it. "Even if he had been a Rose, he wouldn't have matched Stacy. She's not a biological Rose either. Her grandmother was taken in by the Rose family two generations ago."

"I love that Grandfather Thunder knows so much about reservation history and families." For the hundredth time since becoming old enough to want to know more about her father, she wished her father had been from the reservation. Grandfather Thunder would have been able to tell her about him and that side of the family. All she had was a very faded photo her mom said was the only photo she had of Dela's father and that his name was Cisco Alvaro. He didn't tell her about any family or where he came from when they met, fell in love, and he was killed.

"Not everything." Heath frowned.

"I'm sure if he had known how to contact your father, he would have and let you know before your father died." She and Heath had bonded over not knowing their fathers. They understood the hole in their hearts from not having that connection.

"I'm not so sure. When I told him what I had learned about my father, he just sat there nodding his head, as if he knew all the information already."

Dela grasped Heath's forearm. "He would have told you if he knew. He understood our desire to know that part of us."

"That's what I want to believe."

They finished eating. Heath cleaned away the dishes while Dela scooped mint chocolate chip ice cream into bowls.

"Anything worth watching on the television?" Heath asked.

"Probably not." Dela walked over to the recliner and settled into it. Heath hauled his fold-up chair into the living room and sat, watching her flip through channels.

They finally settled on a romantic comedy movie. During the commercials, they talked about life on the rez and who they were leaning toward as the killer.

Her phone buzzed. Dela glanced at the time and the name. 10:00. Quinn. "Hello?" she answered, muting the television.

"Rudy's fingerprints came up as ones on the victim's balcony. He's wanted for assault of an officer in South Dakota during a 'sit-in' at the same time that Tommy Darkhorse and Timmons were there. I went by

Grandfather Thunder's he doesn't know where Rudy is. No one at the tribal police knew what I was talking about when I asked about him."

Dela glanced over at Heath. This wasn't going to set well with Quinn. "Heath called me this afternoon and said Rudy took off."

Quinn cursed on his side of the conversation.

She tried to get out of the chair before Heath grabbed her phone, but he was quicker.

"What about Rudy?" he asked.

Dela could imagine the thoughts whirling in Quinn's head that Heath was here this late at night.

"Shit! I couldn't take him to lock up. I thought he just needed a place to stay. Yeah. I'll get Tribal looking for him. He didn't have a vehicle so he couldn't have gone far." There was a pause. "I'm going now." He shoved the phone at Dela. "He wants to talk to you. See you tomorrow." Heath kissed the top of her head, grabbed up his coat, and headed out the door.

Dela took a deep breath and let it out. "You wanted to talk to me?"

"What was he doing over there again? Doesn't he have a home?" The irritation in Quinn's voice made her hackles rise.

"I can have whoever I want over for dinner. In case you haven't noticed, I'm a grown woman who can invite people I like to my home. And we were comparing what we'd learned today." As soon as the last sentence came out, she realized she was trying to make Quinn think there was nothing between her and Heath. Which there wasn't and why should she care what he thought? She slapped her face and winced. There was still some tender bruising.

"What did you each learn today?" Quinn asked.

She went on to tell him about everything she'd done and what Heath had told her.

"It seems we are all taking different tactics to get to the killer." His voice no longer held animosity.

"I think we each have our favorite for who killed Kevin Silva. Who are you looking into? Connie?" Dela said the woman's name without any inflection.

"She and Wallen are at the top of my list," Quinn said. "This looks like the power company was not happy with an employee and they knew the only way to shut him up would be permanent. Because Silva had a conscience."

Dela nodded. That made sense. "While I think it was a crime of passion and Ben killed him wanting Stacy."

"And who does Heath think killed Silva?"

"I don't know. He's just following all the leads." And now that Quinn asked, she didn't know who Heath believed was the killer.

"Let's all three meet in the coffee shop at nine tomorrow morning. We need to be working together. That way we might have been able to keep Rudy under wraps," Quinn said.

"Do you think Rudy was paid to kill Silva by Connie or Wallen?" Dela asked.

"We won't know until we find him. See you tomorrow. I'll text Heath about the meeting."

The phone went silent. Dela sat in her recliner for another hour, just spinning everything they knew around in her head. Finally, she pushed out of the chair and headed to the bedroom.

After a shower and a good night's sleep, she hoped

her brain would have sorted out the bits of nonsense from the truth.

Chapter Twenty-one

Dela didn't sleep well. Rudy, Stacy, Connie, and Tommy Darkhorse kept popping into her dreams. She didn't think Stacy killed her husband. Tommy Darkhorse… She didn't see him as the killer either. That Rudy had implicated himself with Connie. That was significant. But why did he? Had his high act been just that, an act? Had he been planting incriminating evidence against Connie for a reason?

She parked in her usual spot and walked into the casino, raising her badge to the security scanner.

Oliver was at his post. Many of their employees worked four twelves to have three days off in a row. Oliver was one. On his days off he went fishing.

"Morning, Boss. Kenny said it was a quiet night. And there's a message for you from Farley in surveillance." Oliver held out a typewritten page.

"Thank you." She scanned the page.

I put all the video you asked about on a flash drive

on top of photo printouts of the people the woman you had me follow talked to. Tally marks are on the bottom of the pictures as to how many times she contacted each one. Hope you had a good dinner. Far

It appeared she needed to make a trip to surveillance before meeting Quinn and Heath. She tossed her purse in the drawer in her desk, clipped on her mic, attached the radio to her belt, and shoved the earbud in her right ear.

"I'm picking up the information Farley left for me in surveillance, then meeting with Special Agent Pierce and Tribal Officer Seaver in the coffee shop. I'm available if someone needs me."

Oliver gave her a salute. He had been in Vietnam and many said his encounter with agent orange was why his mind seemed to be going. Elders in his family usually went to the grave with clear minds.

She exited the security offices and stopped to scan the casino floor. This time of day there were fewer guards on duty. However, they were all standing where they could easily see the activity among the slot machines. She nodded to the ones who caught her checking on things. Moving along the wall, she tapped her security card on the little box and the wall opened enough for her to enter.

The four sitting in front of the walls of monitors acknowledged her entry and went back to watching their sections.

"Is Marty in?" she asked, not wanting to enter his office if he or Farley weren't there.

"Yeah," Ike said.

She knocked and walked in.

Marty swung his chair toward the door. "Hey! I

heard you had Farley working over the weekend."

"Yes. He might just be as good as you at tapping that keyboard and making things appear on the monitor." She smiled and walked over to a stack of papers and a flash drive. "He left me a message to pick this up."

"He left me a note saying you'd be in for it." Marty waved a hand toward the papers she had in her hands. "That have something to do with the murder?"

"Yes. I'm hoping it will show us who has been telling the truth and who hasn't." She walked toward the door. "I have a meeting with the FBI and Tribal Police. We'll probably go over this thumb drive together."

"If you need anything else, I'll be here all day." Marty swung back to his keyboard.

"Thanks." Dela exited the surveillance area, crossed the casino floor, and found both Heath and Quinn already seated in the coffee shop. They had folders spread out in front of them.

She walked over and took her usual place on the bench next to Heath.

"You're late," Quinn said.

"That's because I had to pick up this." She placed the photos on the table and held up the flash drive. "Did you bring your laptop?"

"What's that?" Quinn asked as Heath picked up the photos.

"I had Farley follow Connie from the time she arrived until she left. He printed photos of each person she talked to and tallied how many times they met. I haven't had time to look at them."

"She and Rudy met four times according to this."

Heath held up a photo of Connie and Rudy in the Pony Bar & Grill. Four tally marks were on the bottom of the photo.

"That confirms what Rudy said about her talking to him in person." Dela wiggled the flash drive. "After seeing that Spiderman used the fire stairs to get to the roof, I had Farley put all the footage, from midnight until four in the morning, in the hallway to the fire stairs on floor ten on this."

Quinn closed his folder, tucked it into his computer bag, and pulled out a formidable-looking laptop. He opened the computer and pushed buttons. The electronics whirred to life and Dela handed him the flash drive. He clicked some keys and used the mouse pad, before setting it at the end of the table, facing in toward them.

Dela leaned back a little, allowing Heath a line of sight to the video playing. He pulled out his logbook and pen.

"You might have to fast forward," Dela suggested, noting this was a different camera angle than they'd watched to see who went in and out of the victim's room.

Quinn tapped the mousepad and the video moved faster. He stopped it when a person came into view. They didn't go near the stair exit. Several more people came and went.

Dela glanced at the time stamp on the video. It neared the time of the murder. A busboy, or someone dressed like a busboy, pushed a cart down the hall. The cart was left next to the last room's door. The person leaned down, pulling a rope from under the cloth on the cart. He walked over to the fire exit door and disappeared without the camera catching a look at his face.

"His build and the long hair resembles Ben Gibbons," Dela said, her heart hammering in her chest that she had been right about him being the killer.

"Maybe, but how would he get a uniform?" Heath asked.

"Nothing I read about him has him knowing how to use a rope for climbing. And with the time frame, there is no way he could have been back here at…" Quinn squinted at the screen. "Two-forty-five."

"He fits the image of this man. And he could have dropped Stacy off and turned right around and drove quickly back here." Dela pointed to the door on the video.

"We'll get a look at him when he comes back." Heath motioned for Quinn to continue the video.

The door never opened and the cart remained in the hall until the cleaning staff pushed it away.

"He must have got off on another floor." Dela glanced at Heath and then Quinn. "Did your people make a note of footprints stopping at any other floors?"

Heath pulled out his phone and sent off a text.

Quinn did the same with his phone.

"We need to find out if someone purchased rope locally." Dela sat up. "And I need to find out how the killer acquired a food service uniform and cart."

Both phones made noise at the same time.

"Jacob said the downward footprints continued to the ground floor exit," Heath said.

"Shaffer said the same thing. The person left out the ground exit. There won't be any more footage of him." Quinn closed his laptop and pulled the flash drive out of the port.

"Can you get Marty to search the footage of the service elevator coming up to this floor? He would have gone through the service elevator to not draw suspicion." Heath was writing frantically in his logbook as he talked.

"I'm going to drive to the Rose residence and see how long it takes, driving over the speed limit to get here." Quinn handed Dela the flash drive. "You may need this for reference. But keep in mind, at this time it is inconclusive that it was Ben Gibbons we saw."

Dela nodded even as her head told her, he was the one.

Quinn strode across the coffee shop carrying his computer bag. Turning her attention to Heath, she asked, "Were there any photos of Connie and Ben?"

"I didn't look through all of them. She contacted half of the summit attendees." Heath spread the photos out on the table.

Dela started picking up the ones that were a single encounter. None of them had her talking to Ben. She slowly picked up each of the other photos. The last one was Connie talking to Stacy. The two appeared to be having a genial conversation. Dela's gaze wandered to the people in the background. She poked a finger at a person sitting in the booth behind Stacy. "He was here. Watching her before she called for a ride." Ben stared intently at the table occupied by Stacy and Connie.

"Let's go talk to the night managers of the Sunrise Buffet and Stallion Restaurant. The cart had to come from one of those restaurants. The uniform could have been given to him by any of the employees." Dela shoved the flash drive in her pant pocket and gathered all the photos together. She slid out of the booth and headed for the coffee shop entrance.

Heath caught up to her as she made a left to the Sunrise Buffett. They walked by the hostess, through the large room filled with tables and booths, and past the long heated and cold islands overflowing with food. She walked through the swinging kitchen doors and took a right toward the manager's office to the side of the kitchen.

All the cooks, wait staff, and kitchen staff stared as she and Heath knocked once and walked into the office.

Lorraine Tardino, a woman in her fifties with flaming red hair piled on her head, stood up out of her chair. "What do you need?" The woman wasn't known for being polite, except to the patrons of the restaurant.

"Did you have a room service cart missing at the end of shift, last Wednesday?" Dela asked.

"Last Wednesday? How would I know? That is behind me. I focus on what is coming not what has happened." Lorraine's gaze moved to Heath. Her gaze took in his tribal uniform. "Why are the police interested?"

"It has to do with the murder that was committed Wednesday night," Heath said.

"You think one of my staff killed that person?" Lorraine's face puffed up in indignation.

"No. We think someone borrowed a service cart and perhaps a uniform. Did anyone mention anything about that?" Dela asked.

"I'm off at night. The night chef is in charge of things then. He won't be in until three this afternoon. I can call you when he arrives." Lorraine sat back down in her chair as if dismissing them.

"Thank you, I'd appreciate that." Dela led Heath out of the office. "Let's talk to the wait staff. Maybe one of them will give us an idea of what could have happened. The Stallion doesn't even open until four this afternoon. If we strike out here, we'll try there later."

Dela stood in the kitchen just out of the way of the cooks and wait staff. "Could you tell me who is in charge of the wait staff?" she asked the person nearest her.

The young woman pointed to another woman about her own age.

"Thank you. What's her name?"

"Lark."

Dela nodded and walked over to the woman who was counting napkins on a shelf. "Lark? Could Officer Seaver and I have a word with you?"

The woman spun around, her eyes round and worried. "Y-yes."

"We were wondering if you had a service cart missing Thursday morning when you came in to work," Heath said, smiling.

The woman studied the clipboard she clutched to her. "Thursday morning? That was a madhouse. There was a body found in a room and customers were stopping all the staff and asking them questions…" Her eyes widened. "Is that what the missing cart is about?"

"We just need to know if you had a missing cart," Dela said, wondering how this woman could be in charge of wait staff in a busy kitchen.

"Let me check my list. Follow me." Lark wound her way through the kitchen with Dela and Heath in tow. She opened a door marked, employees only, and walked into a lunchroom for the kitchen staff. The woman continued across the room to a desk on the opposite wall. She pulled a drawer open and lifted out another clipboard. She flipped through the pages.

Dela glanced at Heath, who was scanning the room.

Lark walked back toward them with the clipboard. "Yes, we had a service cart returned to us at nine-thirty on Thursday morning. No one seemed to know it was missing until it arrived."

"Are the uniforms the wait staff wear kept in here?" Heath asked.

"No. They change in the employee bathrooms in the back of the casino where they keep their personal belongings. It's safer than here. And Lorraine likes the staff to walk into work wearing their uniforms rather than their street clothes."

"Then you're saying the only way someone could get a uniform would be from the employee's lockers and they would have to go through security to get there?" Heath was scribbling in his logbook.

"Unless someone took their uniforms home to launder." Lark held the clipboard tight against her body.

"Is that normal? Everyone launders their own uniform?" Dela asked.

"Everyone except the cooks. Their whites are washed in the casino laundry. Lorraine likes them to be pristine white and pressed."

"Thank you." Heath closed his logbook.

Dela followed him back through the kitchen and the dining room to the casino floor. "This is where the cart came from. We don't need to talk to anyone at the Stallion."

"I agree. But we need to find out who in that

restaurant would help Ben." Heath nodded toward the buffet. "If you get me a list of the employees from the Sunrise, I can see who I can match up to Ben."

Dela faced Heath. "You agree with me that the person we saw carry the rope up to the roof was Ben Gibbons?"

"It was pretty coincidental that he was the same build and length of hair. Let's get the list." Heath motioned for her to lead him into the casino offices.

Dela waved at her friend Faith working the registration counter. Then waved Heath through the door she'd opened with her security badge.

In the Human Resources Office, Dela had a printout of the Sunrise staff made and handed it to Heath. "I hope you find a connection."

"Me, too. I'll stay in touch and let you know what I find out." Heath thanked the woman who'd helped them and left the offices.

Dela had an idea. "Can you look through the records and see if Ben Gibbons ever worked here?"

"You don't know when?" Olivia asked.

"Sorry, I'm just grasping at straws that he would know so much about the casino because he worked here before." Dela sat down in a chair, giving her stub a rest while Olivia's long nails clicked away on the keyboard.

Dela pulled out her phone to see if Quinn had started back toward the casino, when Olivia said, "He was employed in the Sunrise Buffet for six months and released after being caught smoking pot in the fire stairs, four years ago."

A smile crept onto Dela's lips. "Can you print out a list of the employees who worked in the buffet at that time and then run them against who is still working here?"

"Give me a few minutes. I'll have to converge an old format with a new." Olivia clicked away as Dela texted Heath.

Ben worked in the buffet four years ago. Cross-checking other employees who worked then and are still employed.

Good information. I found someone who works there that was caught in a misdemeanor with Ben three years ago.

Name?

Eddie Spear.

K

Dela reached out for the page Olivia held out. She scanned the document and found Eddie Spear still worked at the casino, in the Sunrise Buffet.

Chapter Twenty-two

Dela noted that Eddie worked the night shift. He wouldn't be in until ten. She left the HR office with the photos Farley had printed and the pages she'd received from Olivia. Since she knew both Heath and Quinn would frown on her talking to Eddie by herself, she decided to visit Marty and see if anyone exchanged a package with Ben that night and if they could see when he took the service cart from the kitchen area to the service area and up to the tenth floor.

She raised her security card to place it on the surveillance room lock pad.

"Dela! Dela, I've been looking for you." Bernie Moon's voice spiraled dread into her chest.

He would want to know why she hadn't solved the murder. Events held here were big money makers for the casino, both in money spent gambling and the use of the conference center.

"Bernie, why are you looking for me?" She

dropped her hand holding the security card and hugged the papers closer to her body as she faced the head of the casino board of trustees. The casinos popping up all over the country on reservations were either run by outside entities or by a local board. This one was run by a local board and Bernie had appointed himself the head of the board. He was savvy at business and knew how to get good publicity for the casino. Right now that had to be hard to do.

"I wondered what you had discovered about the incident that happened here last week." The man drew her toward the Pony Bar & Grill. It was his favorite place to visit with people.

Dela followed him into the nearly empty room. It was nearing the lunch hour on a Tuesday. If Mondays were slow, Tuesdays were even worse. Things didn't start picking up at the casino until Wednesday nights.

She sat at the tall table Bernie chose at the far side of the room where they could talk without the bartender, or anyone coming through the door, hearing.

"We found video proof that someone used the fire stairs to go to the roof and rappel down to the victim's room. That was why we didn't catch anyone going into the room at the time of the murder." Dela placed the papers she'd been holding in her lap.

The bartender arrived.

"Coffee for me," Bernie said and tipped his head toward Dela.

"Coffee for me as well."

The bartender retreated.

"Then you know who did it? Did you tell the police or the FBI?"

"Special Agent Pierce and Tribal Officer Seaver

were both present when we watched the video. They are both making inquiries into who we believe the person to be."

The man's round face wrinkled into a scowl. "What do you mean 'who you believe the person to be?'"

"There wasn't a clear view of his face. But his build and hair kind of gave him away. He has been one of our suspects." She smiled as the bartender arrived with their coffees. "Thank you, Ron."

The man nodded and hurried back to count his bottles of liquor.

"Who do you think it is?" Bernie leaned forward.

Dela shook her head. "No, I'm not telling you. We don't need something slipping out that we believe he is a person of interest."

The man reared back in his chair and glared. "I'm the head of the board. I need to know that this will be settled soon and should have access to all you know."

"You may be the head of the board, but I am head of security. It would be a security risk to tell you what the police, FBI, and I have uncovered. The person has ties to employees in the casino and I'll not have him disappear because of a slip." She kept her gaze even and non-combative staring back at the man who could get her fired if he felt she was being disobedient.

He relaxed and picked up his coffee. "You've pulled our asses out of trouble before. I'm putting my faith in you that you will do it again."

"Thank you. That means a lot that you respect I'll do a good job." She sipped her coffee.

"What's this I heard about you getting caught up in a family dispute?" Bernie asked.

Dela had almost forgotten about the mishap. "I was jogging with my dog and came across a man beating up a woman. I stepped in and kept him from killing her. I incapacitated him and called the police. They took him to jail and gave her a domestic violence advocate. That's it."

Bernie nodded. "It's good you stepped in. Domestic violence needs to stop."

Her phone buzzed. It was Quinn. "I need to take this. It's the FBI." She gathered the papers in one hand and slid off the tall chair.

"Go ahead. Get this solved."

She took that as her clearance to leave. Dela walked out of the bar and grill, answering her phone. "Quinn, are you back?"

"Just pulled into the parking lot. I drove at a normal speed there. I'm sure he wouldn't have been racing with the wife of his victim in the car."

Dela agreed.

"On the way back, it took me thirty minutes. If he didn't stick around and visit after they arrived at the Rose residence, he would have been back here easily by two-thirty."

"Was Ben at his grandparent's house?" she asked.

"I didn't see the Camaro. Can you call Stacy and see if he's still in Idaho with her? I think it's time to pull him in and ask him some questions." A car door closed on his end of the conversation.

"I have some things to tell you. Meet me in the security office." Dela passed the entrance to surveillance and it reminded her she wanted to have Marty pull up video on Ben. She stopped at the entrance and texted him her request.

Quinn strode across the casino floor and swerved her direction. "What have you discovered?"

She finished the text and headed for the door to the security office. "I think I know where Ben acquired the busboy uniform." They stepped into the security office and she continued into the small interview room. Once they were both seated, she sifted through the papers she carried and handed him the ones about Ben having worked at the casino and his friend.

"There is someone working in the Sunrise Buffet who worked with Ben four years ago in the same restaurant. Either he provided Ben with the uniform or Ben had kept one for whatever reason. We also learned there was a service cart returned to the buffet on Thursday morning."

"I'll text Shaffer this Eddie's name and see what he can come up with on him." He pulled out his phone and started typing.

Dela swiped a finger across her phone and called Stacy Silva. The phone rang several times and a man answered.

"Hi, this is Dela from the Casino. I'd like to speak with Stacy, please."

"She's not available," the male voice said.

"Who are you?" she asked.

"A friend. What did you want to talk to her about?" His tone held suspicion.

"I wanted some more information about her husband's fellow employees." She held up a hand when Quinn started to open his mouth.

"What's your number?" The person asked.

Dela rattled off her number and thanked him for giving the message to Stacy.

"What was that all about?" Quinn asked as soon as she'd hit the off button.

"A man answered. Said Stacy wasn't available and wouldn't give me his name."

"Do you think it was Ben?" Quinn asked.

"I'm not sure. I didn't speak with him enough to be certain it was him. But I'd heard the voice before." Dela tried to think when and where. "He was combative at first which made me think it was Ben. But now that the conversation is over, I don't think it was him."

"I'm going to call the agent in Idaho that I have watching Mrs. Silva." Quin stood and walked over to the corner of the room to carry on his conversation.

Dela texted Heath. *Any luck with Eddie Spear?*

I'm trying to find him to question. Heath replied. *Quinn is trying to find Ben.*

He's not with Melba and Butch? He gets paid to take care of them.

Dela stared at the text. *By who?*

His grandparents and the state.

This gave her an idea. *Can you request he be brought in because he isn't doing his job of taking care of his grandparents? I know for a fact he hasn't been there in nearly 3 days.*

That's family services.

A grin spread across her face. Her mom had a friend in family services. *I'm on it.* She texted and dialed her mom.

"Dela, so good to hear from you. Do you have a day off? I have nearly a dozen floor covering samples for you to look at," her mom answered.

"I'll take a look at them later in the week. Could you give me the number of your friend Cheryl at

Family Services?" Dela asked as Quinn finished his call. The line on his brow said his call didn't go well.

"Why do you need Cheryl's number?"

"The caretaker for Butch and Melba Rose hasn't been there for days. They need to be checked on and he needs found." She held up a hand when Quinn started to say something.

"Oh my! That's not good. I'll give her a call and make sure someone checks on them today."

"Thanks, Mom. I'll let you know when you can bring the flooring over." Dela ended the call and stared pointedly at Quinn. "What did you learn?"

"There hasn't been any sign of Ben or Stacy. The agent that is watching them said there haven't been any vehicles in or out in the last 24 hours. And she hasn't seen anyone moving around in the house." Quinn pointed to her phone. "What was that call about? Why Family Services?"

She relayed what she'd learned from Heath and why she sicced her mom on her friend to check on the Roses.

"We need to find him. I hope he hasn't harmed Stacy if she figured out he may have killed her husband." Quinn ran a hand over the back of his neck.

"We need to make a direct connection between the man with the rope who went up the fire stairs and Ben. That way you could get a warrant for his arrest." Dela stood. "Come on. I was headed to see Marty when you arrived. He's following Ben while he was at the casino. If we can catch him wearing the uniform or pushing the cart, then we have him."

She led the way out of the security offices and over to the surveillance entrance. A tap on the key box and they entered.

"Is Marty in the office?" she asked.

Several heads nodded. She took that as an invitation to continue. Dela did one rap on the door and opened it.

Marty was leaned back in his chair, eating pizza. "Hey, I'm still working on what you asked for."

"We came to help speed up the process," Quinn said, pulling a chair up to the table on Marty's left.

Dela took her usual spot on his right. She propped her foot on her box and studied the video up on the monitor. "When is this?"

"Mid-day Wednesday." Marty set down the slice of pizza and clicked keys on the keyboard. The video came to life.

"What was Ben doing here then?" Dela asked as she watched his movements.

Their suspect left the range of that camera. Marty typed and he popped up on the screen again.

"He's headed to the buffet. But Eddie isn't at work yet," Dela commented as they watched him take a seat, get something to drink, and not get food.

"He's waiting for someone," Quinn said.

Five minutes passed with Ben sipping his drink and watching the entrance.

"I don't understand? The Silva's didn't check in until later," Dela said.

A figure came into view. Tommy Darkhorse slid into the booth and the two leaned forward, talking quietly.

Dela studied the two. "You know from the back, those two would look a lot alike…"

"I was thinking the same thing. Darkhorse could

have gone into the room with Silva and back out to give himself an alibi and it would account for any forensic evidence we found in the room, then took the stairs and—" He stopped. "But we didn't see him leave his room."

They watched the two men talk for about ten minutes. Darkhorse stood and left. Ben looked at his phone and waited.

Ten minutes later, Connie Oswood walked up to his table, put a hand on Ben's shoulder, and leaned down, giving him a full-frontal view before she slid into the booth beside him.

Dela's blood boiled watching the woman blatantly use her curvy body to get the man sitting beside her to do her bidding. "What do you think she's asking him to do? Perhaps kill Kevin Silva?"

"I don't know what she's saying but by the way he's wiggling, I have a feeling her hand is on more than his knee under the table," Marty said.

Dela glanced at Marty and Quinn. The two were definitely trying to see what the woman was doing with her hand.

"I'm pretty sure she is manipulating him to murder for her," Dela said, feeling uncomfortable.

"A minute ago you said Tommy Darkhorse fit the description of the person who carried the rope up to the roof. Now you're accusing Ms. Oswood of coercing Ben into killing as if he is no longer accountable for his actions." Quinn leaned back to stare at her behind Marty. "Which is it?"

Chapter Twenty-three

The Special Agent's accusation that she was grasping at straws to find the killer irked Dela. "I don't believe you ever caught up to Ms. Oswood to discover where she—" Dela stopped mid-sentence as she noticed Rosie sitting in the booth on the backside of the one where Ben and Connie sat.

"Come on, Quinn. We're going to go visit Rosie." She put her pointer finger on the screen, showing him why.

Quinn stood. Dela followed, and they left the surveillance room.

Quinn started across the casino floor toward the deli.

"Not so fast. Rosie doesn't work Monday and Tuesday. We'll go to her home." Dela stopped. "Are you driving or me? If it's me, I need to get my purse."

"I'll drive. Where does Rosie live?" Quinn

changed his course, heading to the casino entrance.

Dela spoke into her mic. "I'll be out of the casino for an hour." Everyone on the floor and Oliver in the office acknowledged. She took the earbud out of her ear, shoving it in her pant pocket as they walked out the door.

At Quinn's SUV, Dela unclipped the mic from her shirt and unhooked the radio from her belt, setting it on the console between the seats. "Rosie lives by Riverside. Not far from Molly."

Quinn headed out of the parking lot. "Do you think Rosie will have heard anything?"

"If she did, she'll remember it. I know that for certain." Dela wondered if she knew anything about Eddie and Ben meeting up at the casino. Even if Connie had put Ben up to it, he needed the help of his friend to pull it off.

At Mission Market intersection, Quinn turned left and they followed Mission Road toward Pendleton.

"Turn right up at the next street." Dela leaned forward trying to see if Rosie's car was in her driveway. "Left, in behind that yellow Volkswagen." She smiled. Rosie was home.

Quinn pointed at the two bikes leaned up against the garage. "Does Rosie have kids? She comes on to me like she's single."

"She is single. Those belong to her niece and nephew. She lives here with her sister and brother-in-law." Dela exited the vehicle and walked up to the front door. She rang the bell and waited.

"Coming!" Rosie shouted from somewhere inside the house.

Dela smiled at Quinn and waited. A couple of

minutes passed and the door opened. Rosie's grin broadened when her gaze slid over Dela and landed on Quinn.

"Dela, Special Agent Quinn, come in. My sister is off picking up the kids from school." Rosie backed up, holding the door. Dela smiled at her friend and walked into the living room. The house was small but not cluttered.

"Have a seat." Rosie grabbed Quinn's arm, leading him to the couch where she sat down next to him. "Why have you visited me?"

Dela waited to see if Quinn initiated the conversation. When he seemed at a loss for words, she started. "We were watching footage of a suspect and noticed you were sitting in the booth behind him in the Sunrise Buffet last Wednesday."

Rosie dragged her gaze away from Quinn. "I forgot my lunch that day and didn't want to eat in the deli."

"Do you know who Ben Gibbons is?" Quinn asked.

Rosie smiled at Quinn. "Yes. He is Melba and Butch's grandson. He worked at the casino four years ago and was fired for stealing."

Dela shook her head. "I read he was caught smoking in the fire stairs."

Shaking a finger, Rosie said, "Oh no. He might have been written up for that, but he was caught stealing from the buffet. Food, linens, dishes."

Dela's gaze collided with Quinn's. He could have stolen a uniform.

"Did you happen to overhear his conversation with the woman who joined him?" Dela asked.

"It was the woman you asked me about earlier. The one who was too good to eat at the deli but would take

243

up one of our tables. Yes. She was feeling him up and telling him how he needed to man up and get rid of the obstacle keeping him from having the woman he wanted."

Dela knew who Connie meant. "Did she mention any names or how he could do it?"

"No. She told him, 'He's going to screw over the whole family and hurt her.'"

Connie had not only been playing on his desire for Stacy but his need to take care of family. She was a cold one who used whatever means it took to get what she was paid to accomplish.

"Do you want to know what Tommy Darkhorse said to Ben?" Rosie asked.

"You heard that too?" Dela stared at the woman. "I didn't notice you."

"I sat down right behind Tommy. He was telling Ben to stay away from Stacy. She needed a man who would go places and give her a good life. Ben growled something about no one loved her like he did. Then Tommy said, 'Leave her alone or he'd get her brothers to tell her all they knew about him.'"

This was telling. Her brothers knew that Ben was trying to take her away from Kevin. And they felt her husband was better for her than the younger man who was her own culture.

"Interesting. Ben had plenty of reason to get rid of Kevin." Dela glanced at Quinn. He had a funny look on his face. She glanced down and a grin tipped her lips. Rosie had her hand on Quinn's knee.

"Thank you, Rosie. This information has been helpful," Dela said.

"Any time." The woman's face glowed as she

peered up into Quinn's face. "Now that you know where I live, don't be a stranger." She giggled and Quinn stood.

"Thank you, Rosie. I'll keep that in mind." Quinn strode to the door.

Dela rose, gave her friend a hug. "See you at work tomorrow. And as you know, don't tell anyone what we talked about."

The short, wide woman smiled and pulled her fingers across her mouth as if zipping them shut.

Out in the vehicle, Quinn blew out a long breath. "That woman may not have the curves and skintight clothing like Connie, but she gives off pheromones like a siren."

Dela chuckled. "That's what is so fun about being around her. She doesn't have to flaunt what she has. She just enjoys the moment. That's why I don't care for Connie. She uses it to scheme and turn men's heads so they do her deceitful bidding."

Quinn nodded. "I know that's what she's doing, but she's so mesmerizing, I forget she's a suspect."

Her jaw dropped, hanging her mouth open.

"Close your mouth. I'm man enough to admit, she got to me more than once, and afterward, I was mad at myself." Quinn backed the SUV out of the driveway. "Now where to?"

"You need to send a female agent to bring Connie in for questioning, and we need to find out if Stacy is all right. I'm worried that the agent watching her hasn't seen anything. It's hard telling what Ben might have done if she thwarted his advances." Dela liked Stacy and didn't want any more tragedy to enter her life.

"I'll take you back to the casino and see what I can

learn from the agents that have been watching her place. And I'll check up on the one who has been keeping tabs on Wallen." Quinn drove her back to the casino and pulled up to the entrance.

"Dumping me out, huh," she said, hooking her radio to her belt and clipping the mic to her shirt.

"Yeah. It's easier to connect with other agents at my office. More FBI technology." He grinned. "Are you going to miss my presence at the casino?"

"My staff appreciates when you aren't around. They think you're pushy and bossy." She opened the door and slid out.

"Like you aren't?"

"I'm paid to boss them around and I do it with more subtlety than you do." She closed the door and walked into the casino, slipping the earbud into her ear.

"I'm back," she announced into the mic.

"There's a tribal here looking for you," Nadine's voice rang through the earbud.

"Where is he?" Dela asked.

"Sitting in the deli."

"Copy." Dela changed her course from the security office to the left and the deli. She spotted Detective Dick and groaned. She'd been expecting Heath. Sucking up her attitude, she walked in and sat in the chair across from the detective. "I heard you were looking for me."

He licked his fingers, took a slurp of his drink, and wiped his mouth with a napkin before he glared at her. "I found out that one of my officers has been working behind my back to supply you with information."

She leaned back. His onion breath nearly gagged her. "Which officer would that be? The one who is also working with the FBI?"

Dick glared at her. "I am the officer of record on this case. All you learn needs to go through me."

She shook her head. "I'm not a member of the tribal police force. You can't tell me who to collaborate with. I give all the information I gather to the FBI and Officer Seaver. He has been working with the FBI closely instead of making it a game of who gets the bad guy first. I don't care who finds the killer first as long as we find him."

"Him? You think a man strangled the victim?" Detective Dick had a smug squirmy smile on his lips.

"Do you have evidence to indicate it was a woman?" Dela asked.

"There was hair from two women found in the room. His wife and another woman. I had a witness who said the wife was seen arguing with a woman whose hair matches that of the strands found in the room. I think the victim was having a fling and his wife found out about it and killed him." The detective crossed his arms and smiled at her.

"Except the victim was seen alive after his wife had left the casino." She shrugged.

He frowned.

"We need you in the Pony," came through her earbuds.

"I'm needed. Nice chatting with you." She shoved to her feet and strode out of the deli and across the casino floor wondering what could have happened in the bar and grill that needed her attention.

Stepping inside the dimly lit room, she scanned the tables and booths. She didn't see a single security guard in sight, but in the far corner booth, she spotted Heath and Rudy.

"When did you get here?" she asked, sliding into the seat across from where Heath had Rudy boxed in.

"I spotted Detective Jones' car in the parking lot and asked where he was when I came in. I was told the deli, so we detoured to here and had you called." Heath glanced toward the door.

"I was also in the deli. I'll tell you about our discussion later." Dela peered at Rudy. "Where did you find him?"

"Trying to steal a car at Mission Market." Heath gave the man at his side a disgusted glare. "I have a feeling his 'original' car wasn't stolen from him but rather he stole it from someone else."

Rudy raised his handcuffed hands. "It's cheaper than buying gas."

"Why did you bring him here? Shouldn't he be at your station getting booked?" Dela didn't mind being able to ask the man more questions, but she didn't want Heath to get in trouble by not following protocol.

"I'm taking him there. Do you have photos of our suspects? I thought maybe he could expedite who we are looking for."

Dela pulled out her phone and texted Marty to send her photos of the man with the rope, Tommy Darkhorse, and Ben Gibbons.

While she waited, Dela studied Rudy. He didn't appear to have spent the night outside. "Where did you spend last night?"

"Here, there." The man picked at his left thumb.

"Those are clean clothes. And by the way, they sag, a size or two too large for you." She shifted her attention to Heath. "You found him at Mission Market?

I bet he stayed at the community shelter."

"I'll take him over there before we go to the station."

Her phone dinged. Dela opened the three attachments and pushed her phone across the table in front of Rudy. "Do any of these men look like spiderman?"

She slowly scrolled through the photos.

"He was up high. I couldn't tell if he had long hair or how tall he was." The man studied each of the photos longer than he needed for not knowing what the killer looked like.

Dela made eye contact with Heath and nodded toward Rudy, immersed in studying the photos. She pulled her phone back. "Do you know any of those men?"

"The one was Tommy Darkhorse. The man who got angry when I put a message under his door for Connie." Rudy went back to picking at his thumb.

"What else did Connie have you do?" Heath asked.

"I told you. Follow people. Like Mrs. Silva."

"Do you know why Connie wanted her followed?" Dela asked.

"Will answering these questions help me with the theft charge?" Rudy asked.

"It might help your sentencing if you help us solve a murder," Heath said.

"The other guy you showed me. Connie wanted to know if he met up with or followed Mrs. Silva."

"Just like I discussed with Quinn." Dela shot out of the booth. "Take him to the station, then call me."

Rudy didn't slide out when Heath moved and waved him to follow.

"The man with the rope. He was following Mrs. Silva, too."

Dela dropped back into the booth. "The man with the rope? You know who he is?"

"Yeah. He's wearing a wig and that uniform, but I remember the shoes."

Chapter Twenty-four

Dela pulled the photo up, enlarging the image to get a good look at the shoes. They were a low top hiking boot. She thought back to all the people they had questioned. "I didn't pay attention to people's footwear." She glanced at Heath.

His forehead was furrowed in thought. "I didn't question all the people you and Quinn did."

"Rudy, who is this person?" Dela asked.

"I don't know his name, but he attended the conference and watched Mrs. Silva like a lovesick teenager."

Dela wished she still had the photos of all the people who visited with Connie. She'd left them in the security office. She put her hand on her mic. "I need someone to go into the interview room and bring the pile of papers sitting on the table to me in the Pony."

"Copy," answered Nadine.

Three minutes later, Nadine, one of the security

guards, walked through the door. She scanned the room and walked toward them.

"Thanks, Nadine. Is the floor quiet?"

"A typical Tuesday."

"Good."

Nadine smiled at Heath and Rudy and left.

Dela pulled the information about Ben Gibbons out of the pile of photos and slid the photos across to Rudy. "See if the man who wears those hiking boots is in any of these photos."

"It's kind of hard to look through them with these bracelets on."

Heath shook his head. "You are under arrest for attempting to steal a car. They aren't coming off until all the paperwork is finished."

Dela reached across the table and slowly pulled photos off the top until Rudy put his hands on a photo.

"That's him in the background."

Dela pulled the photo in between her and Heath. The person in the background of the photo was Jerry Timmons. There was even a good view of one of his hiking boots.

She leaned back against the seat. He was the last person she would have thought killed Kevin. "We never saw him enter his room when we watched the video. But when Quinn and I first talked to him, he said he gambled until one. Then when we talked to him again at his home, he said he was in his room at nine. His wife corroborated that he called her from there at nine." Dela scooped up the papers and stood. "I need to go look at video footage." She walked halfway across the room and stopped. "Be careful when you go to the station. From what Detective Dick said, he's gunning for you."

"Don't worry about me." Heath pulled Rudy to his feet.

Dela hurried to the surveillance room. Inside, she strode through the monitor room and walked into Marty's office.

He spun in his chair. "What have you learned?"

"We noticed the person entering the fire stairs with a rope had on hiking boots like this attendee was wearing." She showed him the photo of Timmons. "I'd like to see when he went into his room on Wednesday night."

"Tenth floor?" Marty started typing on the keyboard.

"Yes. He says he was in his room by nine." Dela took her usual seat and watched Marty bring up the hall on floor ten.

"I'm starting it at eight. We can fast forward." The video started forwarding. He stopped it when a person appeared. It wasn't Timmons. They continued until they'd watched all their other suspects come and go and finally settle in for the night in their rooms on this hall.

"He never even went to his room." Dela leaned forward. "We need to discover where he was."

"I can start at the end of the opening statement that evening. Once I find him, I can follow his movements." Marty started typing and stopped. "Do you plan to wait for me to bring him up?"

"How long will it take?"

"Could be ten minutes, could be an hour. It just depends on how hard he is to locate."

"I guess call me when you get it pulled up." She stood and walked to the door. As much as she wanted to discover if Timmons had her and Quinn completely fooled and get this whole thing solved, she couldn't believe Timmons was a murderer.

She also needed to bring Quinn up to speed on this new development and let him know that Rudy was at the tribal police station.

Walking over to the deli, she sat down at a table and dialed Quinn.

"Special Agent Pierce," he answered.

"It's Dela." She went on to tell him about Rudy being in custody and they'd discovered the killer may be Timmons.

"He never entered his room all night?" The disbelief in Quinn's voice echoed her feelings.

"While he is earnest in his job, I can't see him killing anyone," Dela said.

"I didn't peg him for a killer either. But the shoes could be what catches him." Quinn cleared his throat. "The agents in Idaho knocked on the door at the Silva residence and no one was home."

Dread put a knot in Dela's gut. "I don't like that. Did you talk to Stacy's family? Did she mention going anywhere?"

"No one has heard from her."

"What about Ben? Has anyone seen or heard from him?" She had a feeling the man had taken his infatuation with the woman too far.

"He's nowhere to be seen. Neither is the Camaro. I've put out an all points on it. Hopefully, we catch him before he does something stupid." Quinn sounded as tired as she felt.

Her phone buzzed. A glance had her pushing to her feet. "Marty has the footage ready for me to watch. I'll let you know what I discover."

"Want to meet for dinner and see where the evidence is leading us?" Quinn asked.

"Only if you invite Heath, too. He's been working on evidence as well."

"Meet at the Stallion Restaurant at seven?" Quinn asked.

"Sure." She didn't like eating and talking shop in the casino, but it made more sense than driving into Pendleton and then coming back here to put in a few more hours. She had walked across the casino floor to the surveillance lockbox while talking to Quinn. She put her phone away and tapped her security clearance on the box.

Walking through the surveillance room she felt eyes on her. She stopped at Marty's door and did a slow scan of the four surveillance members. It was the woman who said she was related to Ina who watched her. Jacee quickly returned her gaze to her screens.

Dela opened the door and walked through, taking her spot on the right side of Marty. "What did you find?"

"I have it booted up to when your suspect walks out of the conference area." Marty started the video rolling.

She watched Timmons walk out of the event center. He was talking with two other men. His head turned to his left and Stacy came into view. She stood outside the entrance, waiting.

The victim walked out, smiled at his wife and they linked arms. Timmons excused himself from the two men and followed. She caught a glimpse of Rudy following Timmons.

The Silvas went into the Stallion Restaurant. Timmons sat down at a slot machine near the door of the restaurant.

"Fast forward until he moves or the Silvas come back out," she said to Marty.

The man sat at the slot machine until the Silvas exited the restaurant. They kissed and Stacy headed to the casino floor and her husband went into the Pony. Timmons followed Stacy. He sat several machines away from the woman. This went on for almost two hours. Then she stood up and walked away. Timmons followed until she entered the elevator. He walked into the nearest restroom. Dela noted the time said it was 9:24. This had to have been when he called his wife and made her think he was in his room. He walked out of the restroom and back to the machines. He sat at a machine with a view of the elevators until Stacy returned.

Timmons stood and followed her, keeping his distance. Stacy was stopped by Connie. The discussion didn't look friendly. As she moved away from Connie, another person came up and said something to her. She walked over to the Blackjack table where her husband was playing. She said something in his ear. He swiveled on his chair and reached out to her.

Dela was getting the full scene of the argument. She swept her gaze over all the people present. Timmons, Rudy, Ben, Connie, Beecher. All the people who were suspects. Each one of them had witnessed the argument. Who had taken this as an opportunity to do away with Kevin and make it look like the wife did it?

When Stacy left, Timmons entered a restroom, then returned to the slot machine where he could keep an eye on the elevator.

"Fast forward," Dela said.

Stacy exited the elevator with a small bag in hand. Timmons watched her walk out the door. After about ten minutes of staring at the door, he cashed out, turned his slip into the cashier, and headed to the Bar & Grill. He sat in a corner alone.

Marty fast-forwarded. Timmons remained in the bar until closing, then spent the remainder of the night on the casino floor. There was no way, he was the man who'd killed Kevin Silva. But someone had wanted them to think so.

Rudy was the one who mentioned the shoes.

Chapter Twenty-five

"Boss, the Fed and Seaver are here," buzzed in her earbuds. Dela had asked her personnel on the floor to let her know when FBI Special Agent Pierce and Tribal Officer Seaver arrived.

"Thanks, Ross," she responded in the mic.

Kenny was on duty for the night, which meant technically she was finished for the day. But just in case they needed to contact someone on staff, she decided to keep the radio and earbuds on. She left the security office and walked through the casino floor, the long way to her dinner date, but she wanted to check on things before she entered the fancy Stallion Restaurant.

Dela had only eaten in here a couple of times. The food was more expensive and fancier than she liked to eat. But Quinn had picked it, so she'd see what she could find on the menu that appealed to her.

She stopped in the entrance, peering through the dimmed lighting. Dishes clinked, voices whispered, and savory aromas filled the air. Her nose appreciated the herbs and grilled meat over the acrid scent of cigarettes in the casino.

"Dela, I didn't know you were dining with us tonight," Taylor, the hostess, said, smiling.

"I'm here for a dinner meeting with Special Agent Pierce and Tribal Officer Seaver." She scanned the booths near her and didn't see either of the men.

"Agent Pierce reserved one of the VIP booths. Follow me." The woman strode through the strategically placed booths to give each table privacy. In the back of the room in the corners, the booths were even more secluded. That's where she found Quinn and Heath, eating an appetizer and talking.

She noted Quinn had slid to the middle back of the half-circle booth, Heath was on his right and she slid into the booth on his left. "I didn't think I was that late."

"I haven't had anything since this morning. I ordered the appetizer as soon as I sat down," Quinn pushed the basket of bite-sized breaded cheese over to her.

She popped one in her mouth and the waitress arrived.

"What would you like to drink?"

"I'll have a virgin huckleberry margarita, please." She figured it was on Quinn's bill, she might as well live it up. If she wasn't driving straight home after dinner, she wouldn't have ordered the drink without alcohol.

"I'll get your order when I return with the drink." The young woman strode away from the table.

"Take a look at the menu so we can order and then

get down to business," Quinn said.

Dela glanced at Heath who rolled his eyes. She raised the menu to hide the chuckle bubbling in her throat. Since it was Quinn's idea, and his money buying dinner, she'd keep her thoughts to herself about his bossiness.

The menu was even more extravagant than she'd remembered. But she found a baked salmon that sounded good.

When the waitress returned with her drink, they all ordered and as soon as the waitress was out of earshot, Quinn started.

"I have an APB out for Stacy Silva, Ben Gibbons, and the Camaro. So far nothing." The frustration in his voice told her he blamed himself for their disappearance.

"Do you think they were in on it together?" Dela studied Quinn. "Stacy could have been sitting in the car while Ben rappelled down into the room and killed her husband. Then gave him the alibi of having driven her to the Rose's and not left."

"Do either one of you believe that?" Heath asked, peering back and forth between them.

Dela shook her head. "I don't. Stacy loved her husband. She wanted us to find out what happened. I felt all of what she told me was genuine."

Quinn nodded. "I'd follow your instincts any time, but it seems suspicious that they are both missing."

"What did you discover about the owner of the hiking boots?" Heath asked.

"He didn't do it. I watched video footage of him all night. He never left the first floor." Dela thought about the boots and other distinguishing things about the killer. "It's odd that the person we saw entering the fire stairs had long dark hair like Ben and Tommy Darkhorse—"

"And their build," Quinn interrupted.

"And shoes that matched Jerry Timmons." She studied Heath. "Do you think Rudy told us about the shoes to throw us off of him or the real killer?"

"He has admitted to a lot of things, but I agree, I don't think he's told us everything. He could know who really killed Silva. Or who had him killed." Heath picked up a cup of coffee.

"Connie Oswood's phone records revealed she's been in touch with not only the power company she's working for but also someone at the victim's employer." Quinn tossed a paper at Dela.

She noted the highlighted numbers and slid the paper across the table to Heath. She sipped the sweet huckleberry drink, then asked, "Did you get names that correlated to the numbers?"

"I have an agent working on that. Why?" Quinn picked up his glass of iced tea.

"It might be helpful to know who exactly Connie was conspiring with at Hells Canyon Power. Stacy said that Palmer wanted Kevin's job. She'd seemed surprised that Palmer had agreed to help us." Dela sipped her drink.

Heath set down his cup and shoved his utensils around. "You know, someone here at the event had to have supplied the killer with information about the long dark hair, the shoes, and even where to get a uniform and pick up a serving cart. Connie could have done that. Then someone who hadn't been seen here before, could walk in, either register for a room or do the deed and walk out. Without a name or a face, it's going to be like trying to find a needle in a haystack."

Dela leaned back against the seat. "Heath's right. With Connie's resources, she could hire anyone to do the job and give them all the specifics. We need to subpoena her computer. Rosie said she was on it the whole time she sat in the deli."

Quinn grinned. "I already have someone working on the paperwork to get that subpoena." He turned his gaze on Heath. "What about Rudy? Do you think he knows who Connie brought in, if it's not him?"

Dela leaned forward. "How do we know it's not him? I kind of had the impression his coming down off a high was a show. I think he was put up to it by Connie to find out what we know."

"He's not as broad-shouldered as the guy in the video." Heath defended Rudy.

"He could have had more clothes on underneath that uniform. That would have bulked him up. We lose track of him when he leaves the casino, but he is outside, supposedly, during the murder. What if he slipped in, somehow, maybe with the help of Connie? Put on the uniform, walked into the kitchen, pushed a cart out, and went up to the tenth floor."

"Did you ever get footage of a service cart going up in the service elevator to the tenth floor?" Heath asked.

Dela dialed her radio to Surveillance and grasped her mic. "Marty?"

"Copy." Rang in her ear.

"Did you ever check out the room service carts that went up the service elevator to the tenth floor?"

"Affirmative. There were only five that went up

that night and none of them got off on the tenth floor."

"Double frickin' shit. Then how did a service cart get to the tenth floor?" she said in the mic while looking at Quinn and Heath.

"I'll bring up the camera on the guest elevator."

Dela dropped her hand. "He's going to look at the guest elevator footage."

Their meal arrived.

One whiff of her meal and Dela's stomach rumbled. They all began eating and savoring the food. After about ten minutes, Dela leaned back. She'd cleaned up the rice and salmon on her plate. Her bowl of salad and fresh fry bread remained untouched. She'd ask for a take-home box for those.

Her earbud crackled.

"I found him. At two-thirty-seven. Pushing the service cart onto the guest elevator."

She gripped her mic. "Did you get a view of the face?"

"Negative. His hair hung down hiding the side of his face. I looked at the video of the elevator on ten. He backed out and used the hair, again, as a shield. Sorry."

"What about from the kitchen to the elevator?" She knew she was asking Marty to find a miracle. If the man had been that conscious of the cameras to this point, he would have avoided being seen on all of them. Leading them back to it had to be someone who knew the hotel and casino well. Like someone who had worked in the casino before.

She glanced at Quinn and Heath. "Marty found him using the guest elevator, but he shielded his face from the cameras. He has to be someone who works, or has worked, here before."

"Like Ben Gibbons," Quinn said.

She nodded. "Were there any calls from Connie's phone to Ben?"

"None." Quinn shoved his finished dinner toward the middle of the table. He pulled out his phone and started scrolling. "No one has seen anything of the car or Ben and Stacy."

"I hope Stacy didn't figure out Ben killed her husband. There is no telling what Ben might do." Fear tightened Dela's chest. Stacy didn't deserve to lose her husband and be held captive by his murderer.

"I agree it could be Ben given Quinn's figuring out Ben could have been back here in time to strangle the victim. However, if there was no communication between Ben and Connie other than their meeting in the buffet at the start of the conference, do you think Ben was just lucky his shoes were the same as Jerry Timmons, or do you think someone who is good at planning disruptions could have had a hand in it?" Heath shoved his finished plate to the center of the table.

Dela shoved her plate to the edge of the table. "I'll go see Melba and Butch tomorrow morning and ask them if Ben has shoes like this. That will rule him out but not make me feel any better about his and Stacy's disappearance."

"That's a good plan," Quinn said. "And I'll keep working on the Connie angle. See who she was calling at Hells Canyon Power and send a forensic crew out to the Silva residence and see if they can find anything."

"I'll have another chat with Rudy. I think he knows more than he's telling. There was a reason he hung around when all he needed to do was steal another car to leave." Heath pulled his wallet out of his pocket.

"The bureau is paying for this," Quinn said, pulling a credit card out of his pocket.

"I'll pay the tip." Heath dropped a twenty on the table and stood. He glanced at Dela. "You going back to work?"

"Just long enough to check in with Kenny and put my radio up." She stood. "Thank you for dinner, Quinn. We should have this solved soon." Dela walked to the entrance of The Stallion.

She was halfway to the security office when someone touched her arm. She spun and found Heath standing so close she bumped into him.

He put his hands on her upper arms, holding her away from him. "Want me to come over tonight?"

His dark brown eyes peered into hers. If he moved in with her, she needed to get used to his being around. A movement over his shoulder caught her attention. She flicked a glance. Quinn stood twenty feet away watching.

She didn't know what she wanted. "Not tonight. But thanks for asking and not just showing up."

He smiled, gave her arms a squeeze, and strode to the entrance.

Dela hurried into the security office, checked in with Kenny, tucked her radio and earbuds away, and headed out the back door.

It was almost nine. The dark sky forewarned of the rain that was expected tomorrow. The security lights in the parking lot had a weak beam leaving large shadows at the edges of their glow. Walking to her car, Dela spotted someone leaning against the vehicle. She knew Heath would be considerate of her request he didn't come over, so it wasn't him waiting to ask again. The silhouette didn't appear to have long hair. The coat was fitted.

She slowed her pace, narrowing her eyes, and trying to figure out who would be waiting for her. That's when she spotted the dark SUV parked behind her car.

"Why are you waiting for me out here?" she asked when she was within hearing range of Quinn.

"I wanted to make sure you were okay." He pushed away from the car and stepped toward her.

"Why wouldn't I be?" She stopped close enough to see his expression in the low light. Tipping her head back, she peered up into his face.

"It looked like you and Heath were having a disagreement." He peered into her eyes. Concern softened the crinkles at the corners of his eyes.

She smiled. "Not a disagreement. He asked if he could come over for the evening, and I said I wanted to be alone." She shrugged. "Our friendship is strong. I can say no and he doesn't take it as an insult. He knows it's because I need my space. That's what I love about him."

Quinn's eyes sparked and his face became a blank slate, like when he questioned suspects. "I see. Aren't you giving him two different signals if you call it a friendship and then say you love him?"

She laughed until she realized he was being serious. "No. You're smart enough to know there are different kinds of love. I love Heath as a friend. He has always been easy to talk to and we know when to back off and leave the other alone. We had a similar childhood and have bonded over that. When I say I love him, it's as a brother. One I wish I'd had."

"A brother? Does he know that's how you feel about him? He was acting more like a lover when he was asking me questions before you arrived for dinner." Quinn took another step closer to her.

She started to back up, to avoid putting a crick in her neck, but he caught her arm, holding her in place.

"This hurts my neck and puts me off balance," she said, avoiding answering his challenge of whether or not Heath was a lover. She shook off his hand and took two steps backward.

"You're avoiding my question. Does he know you only see him as a brother?" Quinn's gaze seared her with its intensity.

"I don't know. But I haven't given him any reason to think I have any other thoughts about him. When he comes over the next time, I'll discuss it with him. Does that make you feel better? Though why you think any of this is your business, I don't know." She walked up to her car door, put the key in the lock, and opened it.

"If you haven't figured out I'm interested in you as more than someone to help solve murders, then maybe you don't see that Heath cares for more than a brother relationship with you." He spun on his heel and strode to his vehicle.

Dela slid into her car and closed the door, starting up the engine. She sat in the parking lot for twenty minutes after the SUV disappeared. Quinn was interested in a relationship with her and from what he said, so was Heath.

She didn't know whether to shout in frustration or joy.

Chapter Twenty-six

Wednesday morning, Dela called to work saying she wouldn't be in until noon. It was pouring rain, but she loaded Mugshot into her car, muddy paws and all, and they set out for Wildhorse Mountain to talk with Melba and Butch Rose about Ben's shoes.

The drive took longer than usual. The rain was coming down in sheets, making it hard to see. The higher in elevation she went, snowflakes started falling. Her car had new tires. Dela knew she could navigate fresh snow without problems, but the visibility kept her speed at thirty on the curvy roads.

She parked in front of the house. Smoke curled out of the chimney. Freshly split wood was stacked on the front porch. Dela wondered if Ben was back or if her mom's call to the family services had set the old couple up with a wood supply.

"You stay put. I'll be back shortly," she said to Mugshot as she slid out of the car. Large flakes fluttered down, making a white carpet for her to cross to the porch.

She knocked on the door. A television blasted on the other side. She knocked harder.

The volume on the television lowered and she heard footsteps.

The door opened and Ben glared at her. "What are you doing here? You caused enough trouble." He started to close the door.

"I'm worried about Stacy," she said, quickly.

The door opened. "What's wrong with her?" His eyes were wide and his jaw twitched.

"Can I come in? I need to ask you some questions." She opened the screen door and walked into the living room. "Where's Butch and Melba?"

"The health workers came while I was away. They took them to a facility. I'm working on getting them back. When Butch called and said they'd been kidnapped, I hurried back here to see what I could do." Ben sat down on the couch.

Dela sat in the chair opposite. "Does Stacy know?"

"Yeah, she told me to get over here and do what I can and she went to Seattle to find my aunt to talk her into helping get grandma and grandpa back here." He glanced around the room. "They told me they wanted to live here until they died. That's why I'm taking care of them. I was the only one who stepped up to make it happen. Well, Stacy and I are the only ones who understood how important that is to them."

Dela felt bad for bringing the health care system into this family, but she had felt the couple were being neglected. "Where's your car?"

"It broke down on the way back. That's why I'm

stuck up here trying to arrange things with a bad phone connection." His eyes lit up. "Any chance you could give me a ride down to Family Services? I can bum a vehicle off a friend once I get down to Mission."

"Yes, I can give you a ride. I have a couple of questions first."

"Sure. What?"

"Did you answer a call I made to Stacy yesterday?" The more she talked with Ben, she didn't think it was his voice on the phone.

"No. We left the night before. No one should have answered the phone yesterday." He stared at her. "Someone was in Stacy's house after we left?"

"It appears that way. My other question." She pulled out a photo of just the shoes Rudy had pointed out. "Do you own a pair of hiking shoes like these?"

He studied her before he looked at the photo. "No. I own this pair of boots…" He held up a foot showing a well-worn pair of Justin cowboy boots. "…and a pair of athletic shoes."

She wasn't law enforcement and didn't have the right to ask, but she did it anyway. "Can I see where you keep your shoes? And your grandparents' closet?"

Ben stood. "Knock yourself out. My bedroom is on the right and theirs is on the left. I'm going to gather up the papers I need."

Dela stood, waited for him to walk into the kitchen, and she walked down the hall and into his bedroom. It was a mess. She kept an ear out for him coming down the hallway as she kicked over clothes piles to see if there were hiking boots underneath. She found the athletic shoes he'd told her about.

Satisfied there weren't any hiking boots in Ben's

room, she crossed the hall into the grandparents' room. It had the smell of old people. Liniment, cough drops, and stale air. This room was tidy. She found all the shoes lined up in the bottom of the closet. None of which matched her photo.

Returning to the living room, she found Ben standing by the door with a coat on and a file under his arm. He cared more about his grandparents than she'd thought.

Mugshot barked and growled as they approached the car. Dela didn't have any idea what the dog would do if someone he didn't know got in the car.

She opened her door first. "It's okay. Ben is going to ride down to Mission with us," she said, petting the dog's head, calming him down.

To Ben, she said, "Open your door and let him get a whiff of you. I've never had someone else in the car with us, so this is a new experience for him."

Ben did as he was told. His hand shook as he held it toward the dog.

Mugshot sniffed, woofed softer, and then licked his hand.

"I'd say you passed the test. Slide in." Dela closed her door and buckled her seat belt.

Once Ben was buckled in and Mugshot had sniffed his head and drooled on his shoulder, she backed up and headed down the mountain.

"While trying to figure out who killed Kevin, I've learned you were fired from Yellowhawk for stealing drugs and from the casino for stealing food and supplies. Is that why you are taking care of your grandparents?" Dela wondered at his intensity to make sure his grandparents were at home.

He scowled and slunk down in the seat. "I don't like stealing, but Grandpa couldn't afford the medicine the doctor prescribed so I stole some from Yellowhawk. And the food and things from the buffet were to help them along while they waited for their social security checks to start. Once they could no longer work, it took a while to get other sources of money coming in."

Ben truly cared about his grandparents. She felt bad thinking he had killed Kevin.

Halfway down, her phone buzzed. It connected to her car through Bluetooth but when she saw who the caller was, she chose not to answer. She had two good reasons. Ben didn't need to hear the conversation. And Quinn didn't need to know she was alone in a car with one of their murder suspects.

At Mission, she pulled into Nixyaawii Governance Center. "I hope you can get your grandparents back home soon," Dela said, as Ben opened the passenger door.

"Me too. Thanks for the ride." Ben stepped out, closed the door, and strode up to the building.

Dela left the parking lot and headed back to Mission Market. She might as well grab something for lunch and some snacks for tonight. Then she'd take Mugshot home and change into her uniform.

Pulling into the market parking lot, she spotted Grandfather Thunder walking into the store. He didn't own a car and had to have walked all the way. He did that on occasion. Today had been a poor day to go for a walk.

She parked and hurried through the rain into the market. Grandfather Thunder was pouring a cup of coffee. There were two elderly men already seated at a table. Dela gathered up what she wanted, paid for it, and walked over to the table.

"You shouldn't be out walking in weather like this," she said, peering at Grandfather Thunder.

His grin spread across his face as he glanced up at her. "Dela. Good to see you." He raised a hand and swirled it, motioning to his friends. "Delbert and Frank, this is Dela, Deborah's girl. She grew up next door to me. Look at what a fine woman she has grown into."

The two men smiled and nodded their heads.

Dela greeted each one respectfully and returned her attention to Grandfather Thunder. "I'm taking Mugshot home and getting ready for work. I can come back by here on my way to work and take you home if you can wait an hour."

He nodded. "That would be nice. Charlie drove me as far as his niece's house, but I had to walk the rest of the way."

"See you in an hour." She nodded to the two men. "It was nice meeting you." She carried her bag of groceries out to the car and headed home.

♠ ♣ ♥ ♦

An hour later, she pulled into the Mission Market parking lot. She noticed a tribal vehicle parked on the end.

Walking up to the glass front of the building, she spotted Jacob Red Bear sitting with Grandfather Thunder.

Jacob smiled as she walked over to the table. "I offered to take him home but he insisted you were coming for him. I also said I could call and let you know, but it seems he wanted to get a ride home with a pretty woman." Jacob winked and walked away.

Dela grinned down at the old man she considered her grandfather even though they weren't blood-related. "You could have gone home sooner if you had taken Jacob up on his offer."

"But I wouldn't have been able to talk to you." He shoved to his feet and walked slowly to the door.

"Did you need to buy anything?" she asked, noticing there weren't any bags dangling from his hands.

"No. I just came to visit." He pushed the door open.

Dela grinned and shook her head. He was the only person she knew who would walk in the rain to have a conversation. She hurried ahead of him and opened the passenger door. The old man dropped down onto the seat and lifted his legs into the car. It was evident his walk had tired him out.

Once he was settled, she closed the door and rounded the hood, taking her place behind the steering wheel. "Why did you decide to visit on a miserable wet day like today?"

"I had a feeling I needed to tell someone something. And now I know who and what it was." He shifted sideways to face her. "I was to talk to you."

"Is that why you wouldn't let Jacob take you home?" She pulled out of the parking lot and headed toward the home where she'd grown up and her mother still lived.

"Yes. After I saw you, I realized it was you I needed to talk to."

"What did you need to tell me?"

"That man, Rudy, that Heath brought to stay in my camper?"

She nodded, wondering what Grandfather Thunder had learned about the man.

"He asked to borrow my phone. I pretended I only had the one but I went in the bedroom and listened to his conversation."

"That was brave and not smart. If he had known you listened in, you could have been hurt." Dela worried that she and Heath had put the old man in danger.

He waved a hand. "He didn't know I was listening. It sounded like a woman answered. He said no one had a clue and he was getting out of here. That was it. I didn't think too much about it until after he'd left and Heath was upset."

"Did you tell Heath about the conversation?"

"No. He has been distracted. I told him he could live with me, I don't mind, but he insists he will be moving out of his mother's and not to move in with me. But his mother and I know he hasn't been looking for anywhere to move." The man's eyes sparkled. "He has mentioned you quite a bit."

She had never been able to keep anything from the old man. He was more intuitive than her mom. "We have talked about him becoming a roommate in my new house. But it's not finished and after we have a talk, I'm not sure he'll want to rent from me."

She glanced over in time to see the man's eyelids lower. He was hiding his thoughts from her.

The familiar driveway, next to the rosebush hedge her mother planted between the two properties, came into view. She turned into Grandfather Thunder's drive and parked close to the house.

He put a hand on her arm as she reached for her

door handle. "You two have a past and will be working together in the present. You both have good hearts. Keep this in mind when you talk with Heath."

She smiled. "I am only going to tell him how I feel about him. If he doesn't feel the same, then we will deal with the repercussions." Dela slid out, walked around, and opened the door for the old man. She helped him out and up to his front door. "Take care and get dried off and warmed up." A quick hug and she hurried back to her car.

Instead of heading back to the casino, she pulled into her mom's drive and dashed through a downpour up to the door, bursting into the house like when she was younger.

"Oh, my goodness!" Mom put a hand over her chest.

"Sorry, didn't mean to scare you. The rain is coming down in buckets." She stood next to the door on the slate entry. "I just brought Grandfather Thunder home. He walked part of the way to the market."

"In this rain? What was he thinking?" Her mom shot to her feet.

"He's home, but you might go over in half an hour and make sure he put on dry clothes and make him eat some soup or something to warm him up on the inside." She and her mother had been taking care of the widower, who'd lost both his children, ever since they'd moved in next door.

"I will do that. And you? From the uniform are you going or coming from work?" Mom walked across the room and gave her a hug.

"I'm headed to work." She noticed the pile of flooring sitting on the carpet under the front window.

"As soon as we catch the murderer, I'll have you bring that over to my house and we'll go through them."

"I know you have a lot on your mind. If there is anything else you need me to look for, let me know. As you can see, I have the time." She started back to the couch and stopped. "The people you called me about. Family Services brought them to a home to be looked after."

Dela felt bad she'd caused the two to be displaced. "Their grandson is back and he's working to get them released back to him. Please tell your friend that he does care about their welfare." She was beginning to think he wasn't the killer and the family deserved to be back together.

Which reminded her she needed to call Quinn and tell him what she knew. "I need to go. Don't forget to check on Grandfather Thunder."

Her mom scowled. "Like I would forget something like that."

Dela laughed, gave her mom a salute, and dashed to her car. She called Quinn before backing out of the drive.

"Special Agent Pierce," he answered.

"I know where Ben and Stacy are," she said and went on to tell him about her conversation with Ben, including it was someone other than him who answered Stacy's phone the day before.

"If his car broke down, why haven't we found it?" Quinn asked with skepticism.

"I don't know. I didn't think to ask him where. He's at the Nixyaawii Governance Center. You can go over there and ask him. I'm headed to work."

Chapter Twenty-seven

After checking in with everyone at the casino, Dela sat down in the deli after a conversation with Rosie and dialed Heath.

"Officer Seaver, Leave a name, number, and message. I'll get back to you as soon as I can."

She waited for the beep and said, "It's Dela. Give me a call. It's about Rudy." Ending the call, she picked up her cup of coffee and sipped, staring out at the casino floor.

Being head of security for a casino wasn't the job she'd planned on before she'd lost her lower limb, but it had turned into a job she loved. Working with many of the people she grew up with, helping the people who came here to relax or to gamble, and making sure everyone, employees and guests, were safe, had become an obsession with her. This was now her life and she couldn't see doing anything different. It wasn't as danger-riddled as it would have been had she made state police or even a big city cop. But she now realized she was done with danger. She just wanted to protect and not have to watch her back all the time.

Her phone buzzed. Heath.

"Hello, did you get my message?" she asked.

"Yeah. What do you know about Rudy?" He sounded out of breath.

"According to Grandfather Thunder, Rudy made a call at his house while he was staying in the camp trailer. Grandfather listened in and said a woman answered and Rudy said, 'No one had a clue and he was getting out of there.'"

"Why didn't that old fool tell me?" Frustration deepened Heath's voice.

"He said because you have been distracted and he didn't want to bother you." She paraphrased in a way that wouldn't upset the nephew/uncle rapport.

"Rudy was the distraction. Do you think that call was to Connie?"

"The only way we'll know is if you can pull Grandfather Thunder's phone record and see." She became distracted as Quinn and Agent Shaffer strode across the casino floor toward the security office. "Looks like I have company. Quinn and associate just arrived. I'll let you know what they say." She ended the call and rose, carrying her now cold coffee over to the security office.

"Where is she?" Quinn asked in an irritated tone as she opened the door.

Margie was on duty. She gave him a glare. "I don't know. She said she'd be here by noon."

Quinn glanced at his watch. "It's one. Is she ever late?"

"Not if I can help it," Dela said, striding over to the two agents. "What's got your tighty-whities in a wad?"

Margie laughed.

Quinn glared at her. "I came as a courtesy to let you know we have access to Connie Oswood's computer." He tipped his head to Shaffer who held up a laptop.

"I also learned that Rudy possibly called her from Grandfather Thunder's phone. Heath is working on getting a hold of the phone record." She walked to the interview room and entered, leaving the door open for the men to follow.

Shaffer sat down, opened up the computer, and started typing.

"Where did you get this information about Rudy possibly calling Connie?" Quinn asked, sitting down beside Shaffer.

"Grandfather Thunder told me this morning." She went on to tell him the conversation the elder overheard.

"And Seaver is getting the phone records to look for the number called?" Quinn sounded as if he didn't think Heath could do it.

"Yes. Did you catch up to Ben?"

Quinn nodded. "His car quit when he was coming over Tollgate. He said it's in someone's yard. I had him give me the address and there's an agent checking. I also asked for the address of the person he said Stacy was going to see. She is there. I talked to her. I pulled the APB."

"Ya think?" she said, joking.

Shaffer snickered.

"Connie may have instigated the killing, but we

aren't any closer to figuring out who actually strangled the victim." Quinn glared at his partner.

"Forensics didn't come up with anything at the scene that would help?" Dela asked.

Quinn pulled out his phone, tapped, scrolled, and handed it to her. "That's the forensic report. Maybe I missed something."

Dela slowly read the report, word for word. The hairs found had been easy to decipher but they didn't have anything conclusive. "How long until you can compare the DNA from the hairs found to the people we suspect they belong to?"

"Another week." Quinn glanced at her. "You think something might be figured out from them?"

She kept reading. "What's this? A synthetic strand was found. That means there was a wig in that room. Like we thought, the killer wore a wig. Any chance they've figured out if it's a cheap one or who the maker might be?"

Quinn grabbed the phone out of her hand and walked over to a corner. She sighed and glanced at the computer screen. It was an email account. "Anything interesting on there?" she asked Shaffer.

"It looks like Ms. Oswood was working for three different people to keep the dams intact." He glanced up, then pointed to the list of emails. Two of the recipients she recognized. Well not the people, other than Steve Wallen, Kevin's boss. The other was to a man at the power company who paid for Connie's room. The other was from stantheman007@yahoo.com.

"She tells this person to wear a wig and the shoes. And she will have a uniform waiting for him in her car. She also sent him a map of where the cameras are located." The awe in Shaffer's voice irritated Dela.

"That links her to the killer and being an accomplice. You need to send an agent to pick her up for questioning." Dela would have liked to do the questioning but she wasn't a fed or a tribal officer.

She stared at the rhyming words in the email address. "Can you see if that email came from Hells Canyon Power building or perhaps the home of Stan Palmer?"

Quinn joined them. "What about Stan Palmer?"

Dela pointed to the email address. "Stan the man double-oh-seven. If that can be traced back to Stan Palmer, who Stacy said was trying to get rid of her husband, you might have your killer."

"Why would Connie think someone who worked with the victim would be able to kill him?" Quinn stared at Dela.

She stared back. "Maybe his job at the power company was to take care of problems. Kind of like Connie does for the other power company. After all, Wallen did call him in to appease us."

"But he acted scared. He was timid and reminded me of a nerd." Quinn scratched his head.

"If he is a 'gun for hire,' I'd bet he's very good at acting a part." Now that she'd latched onto this combo of accomplice and killer, she liked it.

"He had the other person send me the threats."

"Did he? Or did he send you what he wanted you to have?" Dela was enjoying playing devil's advocate to Quinn's musing. "I would think if he is Wallen's problem solver, he would have access to anything he needs to get that job done. He would be the 'house edge.' The reason Wallen wasn't worried about the breaching happening."

Quinn banged a fist on the table, making both Dela and Shaffer jump. "As soon as you trace that email to the owner, I'm going after him."

"I'm going back to work. I believe you have found your killer combo. But let me know as soon as you have them booked so I can make Bernie happy." She stood to leave.

"You aren't going to tell me, 'I told you so?'" Quinn asked.

"Nah, I think deep down you knew she had something to do with it. And besides. I thought it was Ben before I thought Connie had anything to do with it." Dela walked out of the interview room feeling a bit lighter. Now she could move on to furnishing her home.

Chapter Twenty-eight

Mugshot lay on the floor, staring at the pile of flooring Dela's mom had brought over. They were having lunch and figuring out which flooring would work and last the best.

"I'm glad the murder at the casino was closed," her mom said.

"It's not officially closed. They are still trying to find the woman who helped the killer. According to Quinn, she left the country as soon as they subpoenaed her computer. It links her to other illegal activities. She was manipulating people to favor policies a power and an oil company wanted to be passed." Dela had felt vindicated when Quinn arrived at the casino yesterday and told her about how Connie had run and the incriminating evidence they'd been digging up on the woman. She'd known from the beginning the woman had an agenda and it wasn't for the good of anyone but herself. The toxicology report came back and benzodiazepine was found. It had been a reverse roofie. Connie gave it to the victim so he could easily be strangled.

"Did you get Stan?" Dela had asked Quinn.

"He was picked up clearing out his house. According to the person interviewing him, he's snitching on everyone he's worked for, hoping for a lesser charge of manslaughter. And he was the person you talked to at the Silva residence. He was looking for anything that would put a bad light on the power company." Quinn had even told her that Stan had spread the sage ash around the body after the killing to frame Stacy. Connie had wanted to get her thrown in jail because she was jealous Kevin's love for his wife.

"Dela? Dela, are you listening to me?" Mom asked.

She shook her head, clearing her thoughts. "Yes. I am."

"Then what did I say?"

"Which flooring do you like." Dela hadn't heard a word, but she was pretty sure that would be what her mom asked, since it had been her standard question all morning.

"Ha! I asked when Heath was moving in." Her mom beamed with smugness.

"Why would you ask me that?" She and Heath had a conversation about how she'd told Quinn she'd thought of him as a brother. Even though she still had deeper, lusty feelings for him, she wasn't ready to go there with anyone yet.

He listened, said he had deeper feelings for her and because of that he wouldn't push for more than friendship until she made up her mind.

"Because Grandfather Thunder was busting with

happiness when he told me that Heath was moving in with you."

Dela rolled her eyes. She should have known the old neighbors would be talking about her and Heath. Just like they'd done when they were boyfriend and girlfriend in high school.

"He will be moving in after the flooring is installed. But he will be in the guest room and paying rent. This is not a lovers moving in together thing."

Her mom nodded and her lips remained tipped in a smile. "So which flooring?"

Thank you for reading book two in my new Spotted Pony Casino Mystery series. If you enjoyed the book, please leave a review where you purchased *House Edge*. Reviews are the best way to let an author know you enjoyed the story.

Dela's next book is titled *Double Down*. The woman Dela saved in this book asks her to take the donkey. While retrieving the animal, the husband attacks Dela. She knocks him out and goes home. Later the police arrest her for the murder of the man. Who will believe she didn't do it? Her mom? Grandfather Thunder? Heath? Quinn? And will Detective Jones throw her under the bus?

Paty

About the Author

Paty Jager grew up in Wallowa County in NE Oregon and has always been amazed by its beauty, history, and ruralness. She has always had an interest in the Indigenous people and their culture and enjoys learning more every time she writes a book.

Paty is an award-winning author of 51 novels of murder mystery and western romance. All her work has Western or Native American elements in them along with hints of humor and engaging characters. She and her husband raise alfalfa hay in rural eastern Oregon. Riding horses and battling rattlesnakes, she not only writes the western lifestyle, she lives it.

By following her at one of these places you will always know when the next book is releasing and if she is having any giveaways:

Website: http://www.patyjager.net
Blog: https://writingintothesunset.net/
FB Page: https://www.facebook.com/PatyJagerAuthor/
Pinterest: https://www.pinterest.com/patyjag/
Twitter: https://twitter.com/patyjag
Goodreads:
http://www.goodreads.com/author/show/1005334.Paty_Jager
Newsletter- Mystery: https://bit.ly/2IhmWcm
Bookbub - https://www.bookbub.com/authors/paty-jager

Windtree
Press

Thank you for purchasing this Windtree Press
publication. For other books of the heart, please visit
our website at www.windtreepress.com.

For questions or more information contact us
at info@windtreepress.com.

Windtree Press
www.windtreepress.com

Printed in the USA
CPSIA information can be obtained
at www.ICGtesting.com
LVHW022132130324
774426LV00037B/782

9 781957 638010